DANIEL'S OIL

A TWISTY CHRISTIAN MYSTERY NOVEL

ANGUS REID MYSTERIES - BOOK I I

URCELIA TEIXEIRA

AWARD WINNING AUTHOR

DANIEL'S OIL

A TWISTY CHRISTIAN MYSTERY NOVEL

ANGUS REID MYSTERIES BOOK II

URCELIA TEIXEIRA

E-book © ISBN: 978-1-928537-90-8
Regular Print Paperback © ISBN: 978-1-928537-91-5
Large Print Paperback © ISBN: 978-1-928537-92-2
Published by Purpose Bound Press
Written by Urcelia Teixeira Edited by Perfect Pages Editor
First edition
Urcelia Teixeira
Wiltshire, UK
https://www.urcelia.com

Love may forgive all infirmities and love still in spite of them: but love cannot cease to will their removal.

C. S. Lewis

INSPIRED BY

"Do not remember the former things,
nor consider the things of old..."
Isaiah 43:18
(NKJV)

PREFACE

She should have known. The signs were there, right under her nose, plain as day. Only now, she's meant to look the other way. Bury the pain and the shame as if nothing ever happened.
But, instead, what has rooted is the fine line between hate and forgiveness, torturing her soul with questions forever left unanswered.

And that is the most treacherous tightrope of all...

CHAPTER ONE

Daniel Richardson always knew his choice would carry risks. That his decision on that fateful night would haunt him for decades to come. But that night, at that moment, when the entire building of his life was threatened to be ripped down to the studs, he had told himself that having a choice was not his to enjoy. That there was no other way. That he could live with his conscience. Until the day he died.

And, as time passed, he learned to ignore the still voices within. The ones that nagged with guilt and shame, and sometimes niggled with regret. He knew it was never going to be easy, but now, nearly two decades on, his secret had rooted and buried itself deep into the layers and fibers of his identity to where it had become hardly noticeable.

Even to himself.

Except he had never properly considered how heavy

the weight of his decision would be. No matter how hard he hid the events of that night from himself, he hadn't taken into account that the real work lay with swaying the conscience of those who knew his secret.

PUSHING INTROSPECTION ASIDE, Daniel hastened down the hallway to their small foyer, as his wife's voice came from the sitting room behind him.

"I don't know why you still bother going to these silly town hall meetings. You're only making a fool of yourself," Patty said, where from behind her evening cup of tea she watched her husband get ready to leave.

He briefly glanced at her, knowing the true intent veiled by her words. What she implied was that he was making a fool of *her*.

"They're not silly to me, Patty. I have a vested interest in the buildings in this town and you know it. Keep in mind I built half of these buildings and it's my duty to make sure we maintain the standards that make Weyport a great place to live."

He slipped on his brown trench coat along with his matching tweed newsboy cap, which he shifted in place at the back of his head.

"Had, Daniel, had. You are retired, remember? Your days of having a *vested* interest in what construction goes on in this town are long gone. You really should leave it to the younger generation to decide what needs building and what doesn't. It's not as if we will be around forever to enjoy it, you know."

Daniel grunted as he shot his wife of forty-five years a sideways glance that conveyed his frustration with her comments.

He pulled his hat down over his eyes before he turned to face her.

"It's thanks to hardworking people like my grandfather and me that there *is* a town this *younger* generation might enjoy. They don't know the first thing about the building trade. Everything's on computers and half the materials they use are cheap substitutes. My grandfather taught me everything he knew and quality—"

"Yada, yada, yada, family business. I know, Daniel. No one knows the trade better than you. I've heard it all a thousand times before, but times have changed, and the industry is transforming faster than you can say *build me a house*. I mean look at you, wearing your grandfather's cap and coat like you are clinging to your younger years. It's ridiculous. Your grandfather is long gone, and you closed the doors to the family business the day you retired eight years ago. It's high time you accept your age and fill your days with more important things. Like going to church."

Daniel shot her another glare as his hand reached for the doorknob.

"Don't wait up," he mumbled over his shoulder and pulled the front door shut behind him.

When he stepped off the porch, the rain drenched his

coat before he bridged the few yards to his car. He slipped behind the wheel of his tomato red BMW. His midlife crisis vehicle, as Patty had dubbed it when he first pulled up the drive in it shortly after his fiftieth birthday. It was just another thing for which she had shown her disdain. But eighteen years of her ceaseless complaining about it had long since been shelved, along with the rest of her fault-finding that he had learned to ignore over the years.

Irritation settled in his spirit. Patricia Richardson might have been his wife on paper but that was all. She had never truly understood or respected him like a proper wife should have, he mused. Sure, in the early years of marriage their relationship was great. But somewhere around the halfway mark he had seen her respect for him fade with her return from each Country Club tennis game or women's tea she attended. His thoughts continued spiraling downward. It was so typical of her, thinking she was somehow above him and the blue-collar town hall meetings, as she called them . As if her fancy women's luncheons and pretentious church meetings somehow elevated her rite of passage through life. A spoiled banker's daughter who never had any admiration for him or his profession.

As a fresh wave of rain splashed in his face, Daniel slammed the car's door. He pushed the car into gear and hastily backed out of the driveway, his mood as dark and thunderous as the evening sky.

"Stupid woman," he said aloud, as if Patty had something to do with the weather.

DRIVING OFF, he shifted his mind to keeping the car on the road instead. The windshield wipers were already at full speed and seeing the road ahead became increasingly difficult in the heavy downpour. After a longer drive than usual, he parked in front of the town hall. As always, he was on time but rushed inside nonetheless. He had always taken great pride in being punctual.

Just inside the entrance of the town hall, he pulled his wet cap from his head and tucked it in his coat's side pocket, he slipped his coat off, and draped the wet garment over one arm.

"It's quite the storm out tonight isn't it, Mr. Richardson? Do you want me to take that for you?" A young woman from the mayor's office held her hands out to take his coat, eyeing the small puddles it was leaving all over the floor.

"No need, it's just water. Nothing your diligent hands can't manage I'm sure," Daniel mumbled grumpily.

He snatched up the meeting agenda from the entry table and made his way to his regular aisle seat in the third row and draped his wet coat over the open chair next to him to keep anyone from sitting in it. The hall soon filled up around him and with a slight tip of the head he acknowledged a few passing tradesmen. When he had had enough of the pleasantries he turned his attention to the piece of paper in his hand and pored over the evening's agenda. His eyes fell on the first entry and traced the line item with his callused forefinger, grunting under his breath when he read the name assigned to it.

Shifting uncomfortably in his chair, he looked up and searched the faces until he found who he was looking for.

CHAPTER TWO

B ill Baxter's eyes locked with Daniel's, lingered on his face, and then quickly looked away.

Coward, Daniel thought, dreading having to listen to whatever it was Bill had to contribute to the night's agenda. He had managed to avoid the man for years but just seeing him schmoozing with the mayor made his blood boil. Knowing Bill Baxter, he had something up his dirty sleeve.

"Judging from that frosty look I see the two of you are still at it," Caleb Townsend said as he took the seat diagonally behind Daniel and draped his hands over the back of Daniel's coat chair.

"The man's a greedy weasel," Daniel replied. "Honestly, I don't know how you can stomach working with him. I'm sure one of those big conveyance firms in Boston would snatch you up in a heartbeat if you went knocking on one of their doors."

"Bill's not that bad. Besides, I like Weyport, and I can't really do without his business. Best to keep him sweet, if you know what I mean," Caleb joked.

"Yeah, I'd watch my back if I were you." Daniel paused then continued. "I didn't realize your business was struggling, considering you're the only conveyance attorney in town and all. Business should be booming."

Caleb snickered.

"Take a good look around, Daniel. These people make up the entire property trade in Weyport and most of us are still trying to recover from the whole Covid-19 debacle. New construction pretty much dried up and there are not many property sales happening at the moment either. Haven't been for a while now. Without more development and expansion, it's a matter of time before I'll be forced to shut my firm's doors. And my legal expertise can only stomach so many re-mortgages and deed claims."

Daniel's eyes narrowed as he paused to study Caleb's face.

"Bill sent you to soften me up, didn't he?"

Caleb didn't answer.

"That's what this is about. I should have known something was up the minute I saw his name on the agenda. You playing the pity card is supposed to pave the way for him. Is this about that stupid lake proposal of his? Tell me,

Caleb, when did you become one of Bill Baxter's puppets, huh?"

"I'm no one's puppet, Daniel, but let's face it. Weyport needs the business. More and more families are moving down from the city. This town was bound to grow out of space. There simply aren't enough homes to go around. And if his proposal for the luxury development by the lake is approved, we all win. The entire town wins."

Daniel turned to look at him.

"Over my dead body," he replied. "The ground adjacent to the lake isn't sound for building and Bill knows it."

"There are ways around that, Daniel. With proper drainage and sound foundations, it should be fine."

"All of which will take time and a lot of engineering costs to properly execute. You and I both know Bill Baxter's only goal is to get his houses done as fast as possible so he can get his money and move on to the next quick buck. My family built the very foundations of this town and I will not sit by and watch that man smear my name through the mud. It's not going to happen as long as I have a say in this and you can take that back to Bill to choke on."

Daniel was already up on his feet.

Caleb stood up too.

"What happened between the two of you, Daniel? You used to be friends. Heck the two of you practically built Weyport together. Why do you hate Bill so much?"

Caleb's clever trump card stabbed at something deep inside but Daniel quickly stifled his emotions.

"That man is a lying crook, Caleb, cheating people out of their hard earned money by selling them homes that aren't up to code. You should be ashamed of yourself. Unless of course he's got you in his back pocket to keep your firm afloat."

Daniel's eyes narrowed as he waited for Caleb to respond to his accusation, but he never did. Instead, Caleb turned away and joined Bill and a few of the other board members where they were huddled together in deep conversation on the other side of the room.

"The cheek," Daniel muttered under his breath as he snatched his coat from the chair and made for the door.

But, by the time he reached the end of the aisle, Bill Baxter's voice boomed through the microphone.

Murmurs in the crowded town hall dwindled and Daniel paused in the doorway, curiosity overcoming his desire to storm out.

"Ladies and gentlemen," Bill began, his voice dripping with a false charm that wormed its way under Daniel's skin.

"I have an exciting announcement to share tonight," Bill continued as the room fell into an expectant hush. All eyes turned toward the podium where Bill stood in all his six foot five inch glory, sporting a grin so wide it made Daniel's stomach turn.

Across the hall, Daniel's gaze locked with Bill's, a mixture of suspicion and apprehension in his eyes.

"As you all know," Bill continued, "Weyport has been experiencing a housing shortage for quite some time now. City families who long to make Weyport their new home are moving in at a rapid pace and are struggling to find suitable homes. With the growing demand, we at Weyport Realty have come up with a solution—a ground-breaking property development that will give this town a much needed boost!"

Daniel watched as a wave of excitement rippled through a large portion of the crowd while others stirred with skepticism. He crossed his arms and raised his chin, sending a clear signal to Bill that he was ready to counter his proposal with all his might.

Bill cleared his throat and continued.

"I propose the construction of a state-of-the-art housing estate on the land south of the lake."

He paused and pointed to a slide projected on a large screen behind him. "This development will not only provide both luxury and affordable housing for current and new residents, but it will also generate a substantial revenue to our town's business community. Not to mention that it will, without a doubt, provide much needed new jobs."

Murmurs of approval and dissent echoed through the room as people absorbed Bill's sales pitch.

"What about the concerns regarding the ground? It's

bordering the wetland. Do we really need a repeat of what happened before?" someone from the crowd called out.

Daniel grunted his concurrence.

But Bill flashed a confident smile. "That was a very long time ago and, rest assured, new technology has given us the opportunity to conduct extensive studies. We were able to acquire surveys from some of the country's best engineers and have come up with ways to address that very issue. I guarantee you that all the necessary measures will be taken to ensure the absolute safety of both workers and prospective residents. Once completed, this project will provide a significant shift for Weyport."

As Bill continued, Daniel watched as more questions were thrown Bill's way. But the man had a clever answer for every single one. Daniel's fists clenched tighter across his chest as rage swept through him. This was one project he could not afford to move forward.

Not now, not ever.

CHAPTER THREE

It wasn't long before Bill's practiced charm worked its magic with the attendees as the atmosphere turned into one of celebration, as if the project had already gotten the all clear.

It was as if Bill Baxter had put the town in a trance as they were fixed onto his every lie.

Daniel watched in irritation from the back of the room where he had quietly slipped into an open seat. Apart from a handful of keen birdwatchers expressing their concern over the neighboring wetlands, most of the people around him had fully bought into the project by the lake. Even the mayor showed his support by patting Bill on his back and shaking his hand. The gatherers cheered and clapped as they shouted congratulatory praises at Bill, as if the man was some kind of saint who came to save Weyport.

Nauseating disgust rose in Daniel's throat as bitterness and rage took over his insides.

Bill Baxter had done it. He had won them over, pulled the wool over their eyes like he had always done, and there was not a single thing Daniel could do about it.

He got to his feet and made for the door, briefly looking back over his shoulder at Bill who was relishing in his premature victory. Bill caught Daniel looking and gave him a gloating grin before he continued lapping up the attention with the rest of his presentation.

The rain beat down on Daniel's car as he pushed its nose back home, nearly veering off the road when he took a corner too fast. But the wicked weather was no match for what raged within. This was no longer about Bill winning the hand, or even the smug look on his face when he rubbed his victory in Daniel's face. Nor did any of it have anything to do with his grandfather's legacy.

What had Daniel Richardson's skin tingling and his stomach in knots, was what he had spent the last eighteen years covering up.

WHEN HIS CAR screeched to a halt in his driveway, Patty's face appeared from behind the lace drapes in the window, her eyes squinting into his car's headlights. By the time he reached the porch, she already had the front door open and he stormed in.

"Back so soon? I thought you told me not to wait up."

He slammed the door behind him.

"Not now, Patty," he yelled and flung his wet coat and hat on the coat stand.

"What's gotten into you? Why are you storming in here, looking like this?"

"I said not now, Patty. I don't want to talk about it."

But Patty had gotten to know her husband's moods over the nearly fifty years they had been together. There was only one man in Weyport who could have put her husband in such a foul mood.

"Let me guess. You had a run in with Bill Baxter again, didn't you?" She had the mop in hand and headed for the muddy puddles he had left in his wake. "I don't want to say it, but I told you so. You don't need to be at these meetings anymore," she continued.

"That man's going to be the death of me! He's got this entire town wrapped around his dirty little finger as if he owns it."

Patty set the mop down.

"Out with it then. What has the guy done now that has you this agitated?"

"He's proposing to build one of his second-rate developments on the property by the lake. He had the whole town eating from his hand before his stupid presentation was through. Everyone knows the ground isn't stable and yet they're cheering him on as if he's saving the world. It's ridiculous."

"And what's so bad about that? It's high time Weyport expands. Not to mention all the jobs he'd be creating."

Daniel stood facing his wife, his face as red as his car.

"Don't tell me you're agreeing with this! My grandfather's name—"

"Oh, spare me the spiel about your precious family name, Daniel. As if you honestly care. You cannot possibly be opposed to this. That land by the lake has been standing empty since before you were even born. It's prime property and it makes complete sense to be used for development. What's not to like? The views would be spectacular, and this town could do with the additional revenue it would bring in. I think this is less about the land and more about your ego."

Daniel stared at his wife, the veins in his temples pulsing with indignation.

"I don't know why I thought you would support me on this. You have never supported me on anything. It's like you intentionally push against me just for the sake of it. I should have expected you'd be on his side along with all the other traitors in this town."

He turned and stormed off to the bedroom, Patty trailing in his wake.

"Then help me understand you, Daniel. What's so bad about using the land next to the lake to build a few new homes?"

"The man is a crook, Patty. The land isn't safe. But he conveniently weaseled his way out of that question when someone else who had a bit of sense asked him about it tonight. Bill cuts corners. He's not concerned about people's safety or how this town would supposedly prosper. All he cares about is himself and how much money he'll be adding to his private bank account."

Patty studied her husband's face.

"Why don't you offer to help him then? If it's about building up to code and keeping people safe, why don't you offer to consult and make sure he follows the best practices."

Daniel's eyes turned even darker.

"Over my dead body. I will never work with that man ever again. Never! Do you hear me, Patty? I want nothing to do with Bill Baxter or anything he touches. Mark my words. Nothing good will come from this. Nothing!"

He snatched his pajamas from his closet and stormed down the hall before he disappeared into the guest bedroom, slamming the door shut behind him.

DISBELIEF over her husband's angry outburst and the hatred he had shown toward Bill left Patty confused when she climbed into bed. Daniel had always been short tempered, and a grouch if she were to call a spade a spade. But in all the years they had been married, she'd never seen that much animosity pour from him.

Was there something else that lurked behind his tantrum?

Suspicion prodded at her insides as she tossed in bed. It wasn't like him to not want to see a home take shape, even if it wasn't built according to housing code. Creating homes was his passion. It was as if with each new construction he had given birth to a child, welcoming it into purpose.

But tonight, she had seen something different in her husband's eyes. Hidden behind dark clouds as if it had been brewing there for many years. If she didn't know her husband any better, she could have sworn she saw fear. A desperate kind of fear. And it left her uncomfortable and, dared she say, scared.

Yes, she thought as she drifted off to sleep, Daniel's opposition to the project by the lake was masking something far more important. Something important enough that he would rather die than give way to it.

But the lingering question that played at the back of her mind was how far would Daniel Richardson go to keep pretending he cared more about his family legacy and the safety of the land at the lake than what truly lay hidden behind his fear.

She would challenge him on it tomorrow and get to the truth. Even if he never spoke to her again.

CHAPTER FOUR

As always, Patty woke up at four a.m. When she passed the guest room on the way to the kitchen, she lingered outside the door to listen for Daniel's soft snores. She had grown quite used to his gentle snoring, lulling her to sleep every night and she had oddly missed his presence the night before.

When she didn't hear him, she pressed her ear harder against the door. Remorse for the part she had in the previous night's events suddenly tugged at her heart and her finger gently traced the doorknob. Twenty years ago, she would have playfully slipped into bed with him. But things between them were different now. Distant. Over all the years they had been married, they had only ever slept in separate rooms a handful of times - usually when he came home late from his game of bridge and didn't want to wake her. But mostly, they didn't sleep in separate rooms because they were both too stubborn to give up the bedroom when they had had a spat.

She'd make it up to him, she thought, as she continued into the kitchen to brew the morning pot of coffee. He would not be up until his usual time of eight o'clock when he would expect to sit down to the wholesome breakfast he had insisted was the least of her wifely duties. Then all spats would be forgotten, as if no hurtful words were ever spoken between them the night before.

A slight smile curled at the corners of her mouth as she recalled her late mother once telling her that it was a special gift only men possessed. Over the years, her mother's words were proven to be right more times than she could count.

Forgiveness usually came easy to her so the decision to make him his favorite breakfast was a quick one.

She took her cup of coffee to the dining table where she had gotten into the daily habit of reading her Bible and writing in her journal.

But when she pulled back the lace window covering and glanced out into the street which was part of her morning ritual, her eyes fell upon the empty space in their drive.

At first, she thought her eyes were playing tricks on her but when she looked more closely at the spot where Daniel's car should have been, there was no mistaking it.

His car was gone.

"Thieves!" she blurted out in annoyance, thinking it

must have been stolen since the neighborhood had had an increase in burglaries of late.

She hurried over to the phone and was about to lift it to her ear when she thought it best to let Daniel report the incident instead.

She started calling out to him as she hurried down the hall, briefly knocking on the door before she burst into the guest room.

"Daniel, the thugs who have been going around the neighborhood stole your car," she blurted out and reached for the light switch next to her.

As the room lit up, her eyes found the bed empty, the bedspread neatly in place indicating he hadn't slept in the bed at all.

She nervously glanced at her small gold wristwatch. He was never up that early.

"Daniel?" She called out toward the bathroom then walked into their bedroom on the off chance he crawled back in bed and she hadn't noticed.

After she had searched every room in the house and did not find him, it was clear her husband's vehicle was never stolen and that he must have left after she went to bed the night before.

THE EARLY MORNING sunrise cast its golden rays across the calm waters of the lake and transformed it into a shimmering surface that lit up like a giant mirror in the middle of the expansive stretch of land. Grateful that it had stopped raining a few hours after he got there the night before, Daniel dropped the spade on the firm sand next to his feet then knelt beside it. With the back of his sleeve, he wiped his face as he stared out across the basin. In the distance, the wetland birdlife was starting to come to life, descending on the lake where they scooped down and grabbed their early morning catch. Under a furrowed brow, his eyes surveyed the parts of land he hadn't yet searched, and his shoulders dropped even lower. It was simply too much ground to cover. Years ago he had used the river gauge as his marker but it had somehow disappeared, likely due to rising water levels or storms that had passed through the area over the years. Without the marker it would take him days, longer if he could only search at night.

And time was not on his side.

He squinted into the soft morning light as doubt and fear settled in. Perhaps he was on the wrong side of the lake. It had been so long since he had last been there and his memory wasn't what it used to be. Everything about that night had become fuzzy.

He cursed between tight lips. He should have destroyed it. That night, or the next day even. It was a foolish oversight when his nerves got the better of him. Or perhaps he was tempting fate and wanted to die too. At the very least, he should have written the location down, or drawn a map. He would have been able to find it by now and destroy it, doing what he should have done all those years ago. Before his past finally caught up to him.

But, as Daniel sat there, contemplating his mistakes, it dawned on him that if he couldn't find it, there was a good chance no one else would either. And with any luck, the housing development would never happen, at least not while he was still alive.

He pushed himself off the damp soil that had soaked his pants and dirtied most of his cream-colored shirt. He had been at it all night and, at sixty-eight years of age, his body wasn't accustomed to that much physical exertion anymore. Exhausted, he groaned when he stood upright, his body aching in places he had long forgotten to exercise. He had left his car on the edge of the land and walked toward it, casting a watchful eye in every direction—just in case an early dog walker or fisherman surprised him. From the passenger side of his car, he slipped into the front seat and took his pewter hip flask from the glovebox. It was one more item of his grandfather's he had held onto. Putting the small spout to his lips, the strong liquor burned his dry throat as he drank two mouthfuls before he closed it back inside the cubby. If Patty were there, she would have thrown her scriptures at him.

It was nearly seven thirty. He had to get going before someone saw him. For now, he would leave it be. Who knew, perhaps Patty's God would extend some of that mercy she was always going on about his way and keep his secret buried under the sand forever.

He walked around to the driver's side and dropped in behind the wheel, resting his dirty hands on the steering wheel as he stared out across the land in front of him.

"It's going to be fine, Daniel Richardson," he told himself out loud. "It'll all be all right."

If he had managed to keep it a secret for this long, why would he worry about it now? Besides, there were only three people in the entire world who knew the truth and two of them were dead.

CHAPTER FIVE

Patty restlessly paced the small space of her kitchen. Perhaps Daniel had finally decided to leave her. Perhaps their strained relationship over the past two decades had finally pushed him to quit their marriage.

Her mother had warned her of the fine line between independence and submissiveness in marriage. Daniel was old-school; his expectations of a wife were precisely the opposite of who she was. He wanted her to be reserved, to support him no matter what. *He* needed to be the one to shine, be the king of his castle. And heaven knew she had never been able to do that. Her daddy had raised her to be an independent woman, one who stood proudly and could voice her own opinions. Patty was many things, but she was never the timid little wife Daniel had always wanted. Nor was she able to give him the son he so desperately needed to carry on his family's business. They tried for years but it was as if her body rejected the duty of bearing an heir to his family lineage. And that was the biggest disappointment of all.

She placed her empty coffee cup in the kitchen sink and was ready to store away the delicious salmon omelette she had specially cooked for Daniel when she heard his key in the front door.

Her heart leapt inside her chest as she walked towards the foyer.

Daniel tossed his damp coat onto the coat stand and took off his shoes, clumps of dirt falling to the floor around him.

When he looked up at Patty there was a strange look in his eyes, one that almost looked apologetic, yet he didn't utter a word.

"Is everything all right, Daniel?" Patty asked as her eyes inspected his dirty clothing.

"Fine. I'm going to take a shower."

"There's breakfast. I made you your favorite. Salmon omelette, the nice Norwegian one you like."

"I'm not hungry." He pushed past her, disappearing into their bedroom.

Stunned, Patty's gaze turned back to his coat and shoes and the taupe colored dirt that now covered the hardwood floor.

Fetching the broom and dustpan in the kitchen her mind raced with questions. But none more curious than the ones that arose when she swept the clusters of damp sand into the dustpan. From experience, she knew it wasn't beach sand. Nor was it the dirt that had clung to his work boots when he returned home from a build.

She rubbed a few grains between her fingers as her mind worked through the possibilities.

"What are you doing?" Daniel's sudden presence startled her and she jumped up.

"Cleaning the mess you made, that's all."

"Are you spying on me?"

"No, why would I be doing that? Unless you have something to hide, of course."

She moved past him into the kitchen, her insides bursting to ask him where he had been.

Daniel made a grunting sound and when she realized he was heading back out the door, she hurried toward the foyer.

"Where are you going?" she asked. "You just got here."

"What's with all the questions, huh, Patty? Don't you have one of your feminist meetings to go to?"

His words stung but she wasn't going to let it go.

"Where were you last night, Daniel? And what's with all the dirt all over your shoes and clothing?"

Daniel scoffed. "Since when do you have any interest in what I'm up to? What business is it of yours where I go? The last time I checked you couldn't give a hoot what I do so save me the false concern. You're just looking for another story to take to your high society gossip queens."

He pulled his hat in place at the back of his head.

Hurt lay shallow in the hollow of her throat as she watched him and, with one hand clutching at the invisible pearls around her neck, Patty swallowed hard to hold back her tears.

"That's not true, Daniel. I was worried."

He scoffed.

"I would never betray you. I am still your wife."

"Really? Are you sure about that, Patty? Because last night you picked Bill Baxter's side."

"I didn't pick his side. I was merely trying to get you to open up to me."

"You could have fooled me. You defended him, even told me to offer my expertise to the man. That's the most ridiculous thing I've ever heard and you, of all people, should know better."

"What's going on, Daniel? Where were you last night?"

Daniel didn't answer.

"Why are you shutting me out? If it's about this business with the lake, maybe I can help. The Women's League is meeting—"

"Women's League! There you go again. Always thinking you have all the answers and all the influence. I don't need you to fly in and take over. I am quite capable of handling this without your self-claimed women power."

"I didn't mean it that way, I just...don't go, Daniel. We can work this out."

Daniel looked at her sideways.

"You stopped being my wife many years ago, Patty. Your choice, not mine."

He turned toward the door and left without saying another word, leaving Patty to stand in the middle of the hallway clutching her throat.

She had had every intention of apologizing to her husband and smoothing things over. But this time, this time his words cut far too deep, and Patty could no longer control the tears that now ran freely down her cheeks.

WHEN BILL BAXTER walked into a room the entire room sat up straight. He had a certain authoritative air about him that made people pay attention to him. Tall, with broad shoulders, and slightly overweight around the midriff, he walked into the mayor's office.

"You're still smiling. That's a good sign," he said as the mayor stood to shake his hand.

"Why wouldn't I? This project is just what Weyport needs in the wake of an economic downturn. A little pick-me-up to make this town of ours even greater," the mayor said as they walked to the boardroom.

"Yeah, I would be lying if I said I wasn't excited," Bill said as he accepted a cup of coffee from the mayor's assistant.

"So come on then, my friend. Don't keep me in

suspense. Show me the blueprints so we can get this thing going," the mayor prompted.

Bill spread the sheets of rolled up paper across the boardroom table, weighing them down on the corners with coffee cups. He spent the following fifteen minutes going over the finer details of the soil compounds and the findings of the German engineering team with whom he had been consulting.

The mayor shook his head in amazement.

"I don't know why you didn't think to develop that piece of land a long time ago, Bill. It's going to be an exceptional residential development when you are done with it. Whatever you need from me to help you get this done, just say the word. Permits, road closures, you name it."

Bill's hands went to his hips.

"I appreciate that, Mr. Mayor, but getting permits signed is the least of my concerns."

Curiosity lit up the mayor's eyes.

"Daniel Richardson," Bill informed.

"What about him?" the mayor asked, looking confused.

"He owns the adjacent land and a substantial piece of it cuts directly across the proposed building site." His fingers pointed to a large area on the blueprints. "We've tried every which way we could to work around it but with the soil challenges and so forth, we just can't go ahead without it. We stand to lose about forty percent of the total project revenue, which shoots our profit margins straight out of the water. The project won't be financially viable without encompassing that particular piece of land."

"And he wouldn't sell it?"

"Have you met Daniel Richardson? There's not a chance of him selling, ever! He would rather die than sell it, much less to me. That piece of land belonged to his grandfather and clinging onto his family's legacy means everything to him. He will never let it go."

CHAPTER SIX

Daniel's red BMW screeched into the parking lot in front of the mayor's office. A quick glance in the mirror had him straightening the collar of his clean shirt before he got out of his car and walked up the short path toward the main entrance.

The muscly security guard recognized him and let him in without pause. Inside, the mayor's young receptionist extended a friendly salutation on autopilot. But moments later, realizing who had just arrived, her facial expressions shifted quickly from fright, to panic, back to neutral in mere seconds.

"Mr. Richardson, good morning," she managed to get out. "Do you have an appointment?"

"Do I need an appointment to see the mayor now?" he asked, annoyed.

The young girl's eyes darted toward the boardroom.

"The mayor is, unfortunately, in a meeting right now, Mr. Richardson. Perhaps you would like to make an appointment for later?"

She nervously fumbled with her pencil when Daniel inspected her face with narrowed eyes.

"I'll wait."

He moved toward the small seating area.

"Uh, he might be a while, Mr. Richardson," she said as she quickly hurried after him.

"I said I'd wait."

The young assistant's shoulders dropped in response to Daniel's snappy reply and left her at a loss for words. In a desperate attempt, she looked back at her colleagues, silently summoning them for assistance.

Daniel caught her gesture and studied the faces of her colleagues who all had similar panicked expressions on their faces.

Comprehending the situation, he marched toward the closed boardroom door.

"You can't go in, Mr. Richardson. The mayor's busy." The panicked girl rushed after him.

But Daniel had no intention of stopping and burst into the boardroom to find Bill and the mayor poring over a set of blueprints.

"I should have known you'd be in here first thing this morning to close the deal," Daniel said to Bill when his startled face looked up at him.

"I tried to stop him, Mr. Mayor. I'm sorry," the young girl apologized.

"It's all right, Lacey, I'll take it from here," the mayor announced as he shut the door behind her before he continued.

"Take a seat, Daniel," the mayor invited.

Daniel locked eyes with Bill.

"I don't want to fight over this, Daniel. Perhaps it's time we bury the hatchet. This project isn't about us. It's about our town and making it better. Something your grandfather would have supported."

"Don't you dare speak for my grandfather, Bill Baxter, you hear me?"

Bill's palms went up and out to gesture an apology before he went around the table and sat down.

"Take a seat, Daniel and let's talk about this calmly," the mayor interjected, nudging Daniel into the chair beside him.

"I'm not talking with him here," Daniel said.

"Now, Daniel, it's bound to happen so we might as well get it all over and done with now."

Daniel's gaze dropped to the building plans on the table. Years in the industry had given him enough experience to read them quickly.

"You've been planning this for a while, I see." His gaze went to the mayor's face. "And you've already signed off on this, so I am clearly wasting my time being here." Daniel stood up, a faint smug look on his face. "Well, good luck getting your money back with this one," he said. "It seems by the look of that big red patch down the middle you're not going to walk away a winner on this one after all."

Bill glanced at the mayor.

"You can join us, Daniel. Be a part of this venture," the mayor suggested.

"Or you could sell me your land and do something good with your family name," Bill added.

"You will never get your dirty paws on my land, Bill Backstabber," Daniel said, his choice of words sending a clear and direct message to Bill, that was clearly received.

"Daniel, let's be reasonable," the mayor begged. "This project is one of the best things that could happen to this town. You of all people should appreciate it. Your entire family legacy is tied up in the very foundations of this community. That is something to be immensely proud of. Why stop now? Why wouldn't you want to be a part of this? For our sake and the sake of our children and their future generations," the mayor added.

Daniel's eyes narrowed with anger.

"I couldn't care less about the future generations, Mr. Mayor. That's a club I will never be part of. But even if I had children, I still wouldn't want to be a part of this. I am quite content with Weyport just the way it is."

Daniel turned and walked toward the door.

"You're a selfish man, Daniel Richardson!" Bill yelled

after him. "If your grandfather were still alive, he would feel nothing but disappointment and shame toward you!"

Bill's words stopped Daniel dead in his tracks, and he turned to face Bill, closing the gap between them to where their chests nearly touched. Daniel got closer to Bill's face.

"I already warned you not to speak about my grandfather."

"You're a disgrace to his name, Daniel," Bill taunted, his eyes locked with Daniel's.

Daniel's blood surged with anger and before he could stop himself, he plowed his right fist into Bill's face.

Screams echoed from the back of the office as Daniel's blow sent Bill stumbling back against the wall. An office worker rushed toward Daniel, blocking him from throwing a second punch.

"Daniel, stop! You should leave, before I call the sheriff," the mayor warned.

Daniel grunted and turned to face the mayor.

"You can sign off on his plans all you want, but he will never get his grimy paws on the deed to my land. Never, do you hear me? I would rather die before I see him drag my family's name through the mud."

Daniel turned to leave when Bill yelled after him.

"Careful what you wish for, Daniel!"

Daniel spun around and, like a bull in a ring, charged at Bill. Once more his fist slammed into Bill's face, this time leaving behind a large pool of blood in Bill's mouth and under his nose.

Chaos ensued as the mayor's office staff rushed to protect the mayor while two of his male co-workers pulled Daniel off Bill.

"I'm leaving; get your hands off me." Daniel recoiled, picking up his hat that had dropped to the floor during the scuffle.

As Daniel got behind the wheel of his car, he heard the approaching sirens and saw the police vehicles rounding the corner. A string of cuss words left his lips when, one of the vehicles pulled behind his red car, blocking him from leaving.

Seconds later a deputy was at his window, his hand ready on his weapon as he instructed Daniel to step out of his vehicle.

CHAPTER SEVEN

Daniel didn't argue and stepped out of his car, his hands mockingly in the air. A swift arrest protocol followed, Daniel's hands were cuffed behind his back, and his back was pinned up against the deputy's vehicle.

"That will not be necessary, Deputy," the mayor's voice came from where he stood a short distance away. "We're not pressing charges."

"You sure, Mayor?" the deputy checked.

"Yes, thank you. It was just a minor misunderstanding, one I'm sure Mr. Richardson will come to regret very soon."

Once more Daniel's temper bubbled beneath his skin, burning and threatening to explode at the mayor's intimidating innuendo that was buried in his tone. It was no small misunderstanding, Daniel thought. Protecting that piece of land mattered to him and he meant every word he had said to Bill.

When Bill's smug bloodstained face appeared in silent camaraderie next to the mayor at the office entrance, Daniel was ready to attack again.

But he held back.

Even if fighting for his land robbed him of his last breath, he vowed to do whatever it took to protect his family name. But not from behind bars. Neither Bill Baxter nor anyone else would ever take his legacy away from him, even if the protection of the mayor and all the people in Weyport backed Bill. Daniel would not allow it. Not again. If there was one thing Daniel had learned from his grandfather, it was to wear his family's crest proudly and to do whatever it took to keep their secrets safe. Especially those that could destroy everything his family had built over the years.

As Daniel drove away, he glimpsed the mayor patting Bill on the back in the rearview mirror.

"Yeah, smile all you want, you money grabbing idiots!" He spat the words into the empty space in front of him as his hands wrapped tighter around the steering wheel.

But doubt nagged at the back of his mind. Bill had a lot of powerful people in his back pocket, and since the mayor was onboard with the lake project, Daniel knew he'd be facing quite the battle to keep them from poking around on his land.

Tonight he'd go back and dig until his fingers bled if he had to.

Just in case.

BY THE TIME Daniel pulled up to his house, word of the altercation had already gotten around to Patty, and she stood waiting for him on the front porch. Her fingers fumbled nervously with a single string of black pearls around her neck. Daniel walked up the garden path, his face as thunderous as the dark gray clouds above.

"Don't look at me like that, Patty Richardson."

He pushed past her, and she followed him into the house.

"Daniel, what were you thinking? You're lucky Bill didn't press charges."

Her words stopped Daniel where he was already halfway down the hallway, and he turned to face her.

"Who told you about it, Patty?"

"No one, it's ... it's a small town, Daniel. You know how word gets around. I mean you punched an esteemed member of the community in the middle of the mayor's office for all to see. What did you think was going to happen?"

Daniel closed the short distance between them, his angry presence sending ripples down Patty's spine.

"At least I have a backbone, Patty. If more people stood up to Bill Baxter, this town would have been spared a lot of heartache over the years. The man's playing you all like a fiddle."

He changed direction and walked into the kitchen. Patty followed and watched him lift the silver-plated cloche off his salmon omelette before sticking it in the microwave.

"You're the only one objecting to the lake project, Daniel. Why? What's so terrible about building additional housing that is so desperately needed in this town? At the very least think of your grandfather's legacy, Daniel. You now have a chance to continue it, really cement your family name into this town one final time."

Daniel slammed a glass of orange juice down on the table, its bright orange contents spilling over the sides.

"So, it was Bill who called you. The sneaky snake. He couldn't wait to call you the minute I left the mayor's office. That's low, even for him. To call my wife behind my back to try to get you to persuade me to sell my land to him. I should have known you'd side with him. Don't think I don't know you've been keeping in touch with him all these years."

"Have you forgotten Belinda is his wife, Daniel? I cannot possibly avoid her on the tennis court just because you and her husband had a falling out. And for the record, I'm not siding with him or anyone else for that matter. Like I said last night, you are my husband. My loyalty lies with you, but I also have an opinion. That land has been standing vacant for decades and for what purpose?"

Daniel shuffled uncomfortably.

"What business is it of yours why I choose to not sell my land? It's been in my family longer than I have been alive. Or does that not mean anything to you?" He held up his hand. "Actually, don't answer that. You've never appreciated my family's trade. Too scruffy for your polished upper class."

He snatched up the food and stormed off to the guest bedroom, slamming the door in her face.

Patty wanted to continue their conversation but when her hand reached for the doorknob, Daniel turned the key to the door and locked himself inside.

"Daniel, unlock the door. We should talk about this," she tried.

But her husband's voice came from behind the closed door.

"You're clearly dressed for one of your meetings, Patty, so go, spread whatever nasty thoughts you have of me among your high and mighty feminist friends and leave me alone!"

"It's Wednesday, Daniel. I have women's Bible study at church."

"Oh, even better then. I'm sure your holier-than-thou friends will have much to pray for now."

His words cut deep beyond her well-groomed outward appearance as Patty strolled into her bedroom and sat down on the side of her bed. Tears threatened to ruin her perfect make-up while her insides wanted to yell sarcasm at his face for daring to mock her faith—and eat the omelette she had prepared for him. She would have rather tossed it in the bin if she were honest. But as she stared at her showy yellow marigolds growing just outside her bedroom window, she ushered in a prayer of forgiveness and peace instead.

Since she committed her life to Christ, she had grown used to the daily struggle of being married to a man who claimed to be an agnostic. It was her cross to bear. One she had courageously accepted the day she invited Jesus into her heart. Over the years, she had thought he'd eventually come around. She had hoped that her life would be a testament of faith and show Daniel what could also be his and that he'd want what she had. And that, perhaps by some miracle, the second part of their marriage would turn out better than the first part.

Except it hadn't. Nor did he even once show any interest in her faith. Quite the opposite happened. It was as if the wedge between them grew larger with each passing year.

There were times when weariness had smothered her hope and doubt had found a vulnerable spot in her faith, but not anymore. She was a virtuous woman of faith and he was right. She was his wife and wives stuck by their husbands no matter what.

CHAPTER EIGHT

As with all small towns, word spread through the community quickly and it wasn't long before the news of Daniel's outburst in the mayor's office lay on nearly every community member's lips.

Taking full advantage of the incident by using it as leverage to rally supporters, Bill didn't hesitate to inform anyone who would listen to him that Daniel Richardson's refusal to cooperate had forced him to place the lake project on hold until the city found a way to work around his land. It was a fire he stoked with glee, because, just like Daniel had an idol he chased after with all he possessed, Bill would do just about anything for money.

Bill dropped the bag of ice on his desk. It had only taken a few hours for a giant bruise to take shape across his jaw. But bruise or no bruise, by the time lunch rolled around, Bill, being the ruthless go-getter he was, had assembled a small crew of land surveyors and his architectural team and they were en route to the land by the lake. As they approached the proposed building site, Bill's eyes immediately caught sight of the small mounds of dirt scattered across a patch in Daniel's land. He switched his vehicle off, pulled his sunglasses off, and leaned forward over the steering wheel to have a better look.

"Either this has turned into a small graveyard overnight or we have a giant sand crab infestation," one of the land surveyors commented.

"If it's crabs, we might have the environmentalists on our back," the lead architect commented.

Bill was already out of his car and walked over to one of the closest mounds. He kicked the small heap of sand with his shoe then squatted next to the small hole.

"It's definitely not sea turtles. It's too far off the beach for that," he observed, walking to the next one, then the next, inspecting each one of the holes that roughly resembled the same size and depth.

"It's almost as if someone's been digging for treasure," another remarked. The small group of men exploded into laughter.

Bill stood back, hands on hips as he scanned across the land.

"I don't think he's far off, actually. The holes are condensed to one area so whoever's been digging these holes was looking for something specific. And interestingly enough, it appears to only be on Daniel's stretch of land."

"We're going to have to rule out the possibility of it being crabs or, crazy as it might seem, any other material that might prevent us from using the land," the architect answered.

Bill frowned.

"Like what? Gold? That's ridiculous."

"Is it? You did say this land has been in the Richardson family for decades. Perhaps Daniel Richardson knows something we don't. It's no secret that prospectors have been searching parts of the U.S. Coastline for metals since the early 1800s. That would certainly explain why he's so protective over the land."

The small group paused in quiet contemplation before one of the surveyors said, "We can always run a LiDAR across the area if you want. I can have one here within the hour."

"What's a LiDAR?" Bill asked.

"It's a scanner that uses the light from a laser to collect both subterranean and surface measurements. Essentially, it will create a 3D model and map of any objects found beneath the surface," the team member answered.

"You think it will find whatever they were looking for." Bill asked again.

"I do. If it's still here of course. It's accurate up to a quarter of an inch so if there is something here, we will find it. We can double up with a metal detector but of course that'll only work if the object is made of metal. And without the necessary permits, we'd have to stay clear of Richardson's land but, we can certainly scan around it."

Bill nodded.

"Let's do it. But to stay ahead of the game, we'll go over the blueprints to see if there's a way we can work around including his land in the development."

The team agreed and while they waited for the LiDAR scanner to arrive, they surveyed the land and discussed possible ways to go ahead with the lake project without having to include Daniel's land.

A little over an hour later, a member of the surveyor's team arrived back on site with both a LiDAR scanner and two metal detectors in hand.

While Bill and his architect pored over the blueprints with mounting frustration, the rest of the team got to work with the scanners. But several hours later, their efforts had yielded no success as it became clear that without Daniel's land, the lake project could not continue.

Bill's patience was wearing thin. He had a lot riding on this project. In fact, his entire business was at stake, something he had managed to keep hidden for several years. The fake it until you make it mentality had gotten him this far. If he could make it in New York's competitive real estate market, he could make it anywhere, and not Daniel or anyone else was going to stand in his way. He had come too far to see it all go up in smoke because of a selfish old man's half-baked legacy.

Bill's shoulders pulled back as he straightened his

spine and quietly recited his daily affirmations in his head. He glanced across the expansive basin. There was only one person who would dig that many holes in one concentrated piece of land. And if he knew Daniel - and he did - he would go to great lengths to protect his grandfather and their family name.

"Expand the search boys. I don't care what it takes. I want every square inch of this property scanned. From the trees out to the lake and up to the edge of Daniel's property," he announced with new vigor in his belly. "If Daniel Richardson is hiding something on this land I want to know what it is."

Dollar signs flashed before Bill's eyes and his skin tingled as he waited for his team to find something. It was as if his body had come alive at the prospect of making more money off this land than a few luxury condominiums could make him in a lifetime.

But more than the exhilarating feeling of living a life of riches, nothing compared to the satisfaction he'd get from being one up on Daniel. From beating Daniel at his own game. A giant grin stretched across his face as he soaked in the premature victory, shutting his eyes to take in the afternoon glow, as if the amber light somehow cloaked him in affluence.

If Daniel's land contained his ticket to freedom, a one-way ticket to wealth, the dream he'd been chasing since he was thirteen, he'd go to any lengths to take what the universe owed him.

CHAPTER NINE

I t was early evening when Daniel finally decided to
come out of hiding after spending the entire day in the
guest bedroom.

Patty had tried to offer him lunch, as a way of
extending an olive branch, but he flat out ignored her. At
one point, she was certain she'd heard him sleeping, which
was very unlike her husband of nearly fifty years. Never
during their entire marriage had he ever taken a nap in the
middle of the day. Not even when he had pneumonia from
the time he pushed to finish a project in the middle of
winter. He had always said sleeping during the day was
for lazy people.

But she also knew this wasn't like any other day. Something about Daniel was different. Something between
them had changed.

She had been pacing the hallway all day, a restlessness

rooted in her spirit telling her that something was terribly wrong. Even way back, when she had first suspected his midlife crisis drove him into the arms of another woman, even then she hadn't felt this restless.

She pressed her ear against the guest bedroom door. First, there was quiet, and then she heard the wood of the bed frame creaking. Panic surged through her. If he caught her lingering outside his door, he would get mad. She heard him shuffling toward the door and spun around as quickly and quietly as the floorboards would allow, but it was too late.

He yanked the door open and caught her mid-spin.

"What are you doing sneaking around outside my room? I don't need a babysitter, Patty," Daniel said grumpily.

Patty's voice quivered a faint reply.

"I was getting worried, is all. You never sleep during the day. Are you feeling unwell?"

He shot her an irritated look as he rolled his eyes then pushed past her to the bathroom and shut the door in her face.

Patty hovered in the hallway for the briefest of moments, tears lodged deep in her throat. As she walked over to the kitchen and popped the kettle on the stove, her mind raced with questions. What could she possibly have done that made him so distant from her? He had accused her of siding with Bill. Over what, the lake project? It just didn't make any sense to her. This entire ordeal around the land by the lake was absurd - land that he inherited through the family business and on which he had never expressed any interest in developing.

Lost in her confused thoughts, she didn't hear Daniel come into the kitchen until he plonked a thermos down next to her and filled it with hot water.

Careful not to further upset him, she kept quiet and pretended to be busy with making her tea. Silence wedged a giant chasm between them.

Patty played around with her teabag, her mind begging God to show her what to do or say.

But God was silent, and experience had taught her not to lean into her own flesh in situations like these but to instead wait until words came to her.

The silence continued for a while and Patty decided to get started on dinner.

"Don't bother. I'm going out," Daniel interrupted when he saw her taking out the skillet.

Confusion made it to Patty's face.

"Out? What do you mean? It's not bridge night, is it?" She glanced at the calendar on the refrigerator and saw that it wasn't.

"I don't need to tell you where I'm going. I don't answer to you, Patty."

She took a deep breath.

"Why are you being so mean to me, Daniel? What have I done for you to push me aside like a dirty rag?"

Daniel dropped a sandwich and a few pieces of fruit in a paper bag and turned to leave.

"Daniel! I'm talking to you. I deserve an answer."

He turned his body halfway, conveying that he wouldn't entirely open up to her.

"It's what you haven't done, Patty," he said then walked toward the front door, Patty running after him.

"What does that mean? I don't understand." She could no longer keep her emotions at bay and buried her face in her pink and blue peony-printed apron.

Her sudden unraveling made him stop and he stood in front of the door, rolling his hat between his calloused fingers.

"You've never supported me in anything I do or believe in. It's always just been about you - your faith, your church meetings, your ladies' luncheons, you. And I've always supported you in everything, provided for you. But you've been so caught up in appearances and your social diary that you've neglected me, your husband, us."

Patty's hands went to her neck as she listened and let him continue.

"I've never been good enough for you. You lost interest in me twenty years ago."

Patty searched her memories to around the time he turned fifty and he came home with his flashy red car.

"I never asked you to change and buy fancy cars, Daniel."

"You didn't have to. Besides, you were too busy socializing with the town's elite to even notice me. To notice that I needed help with the family business."

She paused briefly, her fingers playing with the lace frill on her apron.

"Is that why you had an affair?" she asked with caution. It was the first time she had ever mentioned the affair to him.

Daniel looked shocked and uncomfortable.

"Yes, I knew about the affair, Daniel. I just always prayed you would come to your senses and stop. And then you did, around the time your grandfather passed."

"But none of that matters anymore. I've tried to be a better wife to you after all that but it's as if something was broken between us. I've been trying to fix it ever since."

As Patty talked, Daniel's face became grimmer by the second until he pulled his cap on and grabbed his keys off the foyer table.

"Daniel, don't leave, please," she begged as she approached him. "We're finally talking. Don't leave now. We can fix this. I promise I'll support you more, no matter what."

But Daniel had turned his back on her, his hands fumbling with the latch on the door.

"Don't wait up," he mumbled and walked outside.

Patty followed him out onto the porch, desperate to continue their conversation. She caught sight of the fast approaching thunder clouds over the treetops near the house.

"Daniel, please don't leave. There's a storm coming, it's too dangerous for you to be out on the road in this weather. It's going to be dark soon. What if you get stuck somewhere or worse, crash your car?"

He briefly turned back to look at her.

"Well, then I guess you are finally rid of me and my flashy red car."

His callous words rendered Patty mute and she watched Daniel get into his car and drive away. Moments later a bolt of lightning flashed across the stormy sky and thunder clapped barely a second later.

The loud noise snapped her back into the present and she ran for shelter inside the house, leaning back against the closed door as soon as she stepped inside.

She desperately wanted to cry, needed to cry, but for reasons unknown to her, all she felt was numbness, as if her body had gone into shock. As if it knew before her mind did that something horrible was coming.

CHAPTER TEN

Angus Reid rustled the pages of the morning newspaper and folded it in half before dropping it on the diner table next to his half empty cup of coffee. He glanced at his watch and realized Murphy was nearly twenty minutes late.

"Is Dr. Delaney not joining you this morning, Sheriff?" Monica asked when she filled his cup with fresh coffee.

"I'm not sure. Can we give it a few more minutes? I'm sure she's on her way."

"Of course. I'll keep an eye out for her." She smiled a mischievous smile. "You make a great couple," she added.

"Thanks, Monica, but a handful of diner breakfasts hardly means we're a couple. We're just two people getting to know each other," Angus responded.

"Ah, you two are a match made in heaven, Sheriff.

Take it from me. I've worked here long enough to know a good thing when I see it,"Monica said, turning her attention to another table.

"I'll get Mo to start your pancakes so long, Sheriff," she announced over her shoulder as she scooted off to her next table.

"Sorry I'm late, Angus," Murphy said, rushing in from behind and gently brushing against his arm before she sat down opposite him.

"I had a late night finishing up my research papers for the upcoming symposium and totally lost track of time this morning. I cannot believe it's only a week away. I feel like I'm not properly prepared."

"You will be just fine, Murphy. You are one of the best medical examiners I have ever met. I'm sure they'll be hanging on to your every word."

"I hope you're right."

She signaled her arrival to Monica.

"Anyway, anything interesting happening on your end?" She continued as she slipped off her coat.

"Nothing much, thankfully. The town seems to be behaving at the moment. A few domestic disputes and a spate of car break-ins that I think we have a handle on but other than that, I'm in a quiet spell."

"May that last! We know that somehow it's always calmest before the storm. Speaking of, how bad was that storm last night?"

"The worst I've seen in a long while. Apparently,

fallen trees are blocking a few of the roads. Let's hope no one got hurt," Murphy said.

Monica was back with Murphy's lemon tea.

"Morning, Dr. Delaney. The usual?" the waitress checked as she popped a plate of homemade pancakes and crispy bacon in front of Angus.

"That would be great. Thank you, Monica."

"Coming right up."

Murphy watched as Angus drizzled a generous helping of maple syrup over his bacon.

"Want some?" Angus offered as Murphy took a sip of her tea.

"And clog up my arteries? No thanks."

Angus took a large bite and teased her with a humming sound.

"Very funny. You know that stuff can kill you, right?"

"Is that what your corpses have been telling you?"

"It's a fact. Heart attacks are the number one cause of death in people who consume too much fat and sugar."

Angus looked up at her, a forkful of food paused in front of his mouth.

"Well, if I do suffer a heart attack from eating Mo's delicious breakfasts every morning, I'll know I'll have the best ME in town to give me a proper sendoff."

Murphy blushed.

"Flattery will get you everywhere, Sheriff. I'm also the only ME in town," she said, winking. "But it's no laughing matter, Angus. I'd rather you live than tempt fate and die an early death."

"And I appreciate you, Murphy, but once you taste Mo's pancakes even you will have a tough time saying no to them."

"Ugh, you're impossible," she said then changed the topic.

"What do you make of this business over the lake project?" She inclined her chin, pointing to the newspaper next to him as Monica delivered her poached eggs and spinach.

"I'm still trying to make sense of it all. There's so much gossip flying about that I can't get to the bottom of it."

"Oh, this mess goes back years, decades even. Daniel Richardson and Bill Baxter were business partners back in the day. The two were on fire, building most of the houses you see in and around Weyport. Daniel's grandfather was one of the founders of Weyport. He had made quite a name for himself, actually. The construction business was passed down to Daniel when the old man finally died at ninety-four about fifteen years ago. Seemingly, as fit as a fiddle so the cardiac arrest came out of nowhere. That man lived for his construction projects and took great pride in his old-school workmanship. Daniel inherited everything, following in his footsteps until he retired."

"And Daniel's father? Where was he in all this?"

She shook her head and paused to take two sips of her tea.

"Legend has it that his father died when Daniel was a young boy. The roof of one of the housing projects they were working on collapsed on him. As far as I know it was an accident. People say that's what pushed Daniel's grandfather over the edge. Apparently, the old man went a bit bonkers after that. His need to have the reputation of building quality homes intensified. Even with his short temper he was in great demand and worked non-stop."

"And Daniel's mother? Is she still alive?"

Murphy shook her head, pausing to finish a bit of food before she answered.

"His grandfather raised him. Daniel's mother died a few days after giving birth to him. Sickle cell disease, as far as I know. She didn't know she had it until she gave birth. Luckily, Daniel's grandfather was still in his forties; he married really young, so he jumped straight into raising Daniel as if he was his own son."

"Sounds like Daniel had a tough childhood. What about this Bill fellow?"

"Oh, Bill is a real piece of work. He was a boy genius who made a name for himself in New York before moving here to open up his own real estate company. He has a knack for selling just about anything and has quite the Rolodex of contacts in his arsenal. He's as sly as they come. If you ever buy a house from him, make sure to read the fine print."

"Noted. So, what happened that led to the two hating each other's guts?"

Murphy swallowed another mouthful of tea.

"That's the question on everyone's lips these days. One minute they were making a killing together and the next minute they were enemies. I don't think Patty Richardson even knows what happened between them. Whatever it was must have been a big deal for Daniel to summarily shut down his family business and retire. I'm surprised they still live in the same town."

"It's that bad?"

She nodded, her eyes wide as she finished a bite of food.

"I'm confused. If that's all that happened, and it was how long ago?"

"About eight years. Although people are saying it was a long time coming."

"Then why not just leave it at that? What does all that drama have to do with the lake project and Daniel attacking Bill?"

Murphy shrugged her shoulders.

"I don't know. There's a lot of talk going around but you know this town. People tend to embellish things to make life more interesting. All I know is that Bill's been dropping little hints about the entire project hinging on some piece of land they're hoping to acquire. And if this town's gossip is anything to go by, the land in question belongs to none other than Daniel Richardson."

CHAPTER ELEVEN

Angus chuckled with sarcasm.

"Of course, the land belongs to Daniel. That's the law of nature having its satirical stab. Well, let's hope they come to some kind of an agreement very soon and get this project going because I've still not managed to find a permanent place to live. The Airbnb is pleasant but it would be great to have a bit more space around me and a permanent address. Perhaps even get a dog and start a veggie patch."

Murphy cocked her head.

"I'm not surprised about you wanting a dog but I didn't know you had green thumbs, Sheriff."

"I don't," he laughed, "but I've always dreamed of having my own house where I can settle down. Back in Vegas, I was in a third floor apartment and far too busy climbing the corporate ladder to mess around with even a balcony garden.But now I feel like I finally have the chance to make a home for myself."

"I'm sure something is bound to pop up soon enough. I'll keep my ears open for you."

Angus' mobile phone vibrated on the table in front of him and he took a quick look at the message that came in.

"So much for an easy work schedule." He glanced at Murphy and held up a finger. "Wait for it..."

Murphy's cellphone rang two seconds later, and she took a quick look at the screen before she answered the call.

"And there it is," Angus muttered, shaking his head as he responded to his text message.

"Well, I guess our breakfast is over, Sheriff. Duty calls," Murphy said as she hung up.

"Yup. Seems you're about to get a John or Jane Doe on your table this morning."

"What's left of it, yes."

"What's left of it?"

"Yeah, apparently the body is a mess. Sounds like I'll have a body bag of mostly bones and juices to work through."

"Sounds fascinating," Angus said sarcastically as he hastily worked through his breakfast.

"Fine, I'll spare you the graphics. I wouldn't want to spoil your healthy breakfast," she quipped. "Besides, I guess you'll see it for yourself soon enough."

He smiled.

"My deputy tells me the body was found inside a barrel, buried in the foundations of a house on the other side of town."

"That's startling. I mean, who'd do such an evil thing?"

Angus gulped the last bit of his breakfast down with two successive forkfuls and washed it down with the last of his coffee, pushing his empty plate aside.

Murphy did the same then said, "I suppose this means that your *quiet spell* has come to an abrupt end. Sounds like quite the murder case to me. I mean it's not every day a body in a barrel surfaces."

"We had better get going," he said. "We have a murderer to hunt down, Doc."

"Agreed, I'll try my best to identify the body as soon as I can. With any luck, I'll have a few teeth to match to dental records so I can get you a name. But don't hold your breath, Angus. It sounds like I'll have to pull out all the stops on this one. They tell me it is, for lack of a better term, pretty much liquified."

WHEN ANGUS and Murphy arrived at the scene, they found the undersheriff interrogating a man dressed like he had just stepped out of a western movie.

"That must be our owner," Angus said as they walked over.

Spotting their arrival, Miguel handed his questioning

over to one of the other deputies and pulled Angus and Murphy aside.

"What are we looking at here?" Angus asked him.

Miguel looked at Murphy.

"You're going to have your hands full with this one, Doc. It's not the prettiest of corpses I've ever seen. Looks like it might better suit a zombie apocalypse movie than your morgue." He pointed to the side of the property. "It's around the back."

Once Murphy left, Angus took in the scene.

"It's hardly a house, Miguel. Looks more like a building site. I'm assuming our cowboy over there is the owner."

"Affirmative, his name is Rowley Digby. He's a writer from Nashville. I've never heard of the guy but then again I'm not much of a reader."

"And what's the deal with this property?"

"The guy says he just inherited it from his uncle about six months ago. Says he's been here twice before today; the first time after he was informed of his inheritance and the second time with an architect. He says he had plans to turn it into a vacation spot. Now all he wants to do is sell it."

"So, it's mid renovation."

"That's how they discovered the body. The construction workers found the barrel yesterday but the storm grounded all incoming planes last night, so Digby could only fly in this morning. He says he took one look inside this morning and reported it right away. I've already called the airline and confirmed he had a seat booked on the red-eye last night but got stranded at the airport until the storm passed and he took the first flight out this morning. I'm waiting for the airline to get back to me with his flight history over the last six months, although we might need to go way back by the looks of the corpse. Tammy's tracking down details around the deed and the supposed inheritance."

Angus smiled at Miguel, a proud expression in his eyes.

"You're turning out to be a great undersheriff, Miguel."

Miguel's face lit up.

"Thanks, Sheriff."

"Just don't come for my job."

"Don't worry, your job is safe. If I do move up the line, I'd like it to be closer to home. Most of my family is in San Antonio."

"Duly noted. Wanna show me what this body in a barrel looks like then?"

Miguel took Angus along the side of the property to the back of the house where most of the back elevation had been stripped down to its foundations.

They found Murphy overseeing the extraction of the body from a barrel that had been lifted out of a hole in the concrete floor.

A putrid smell lay thick in the air and Angus quickly buried his nose in the crook of his elbow.

"I warned you it wasn't pretty, Sheriff," Miguel said from behind a cupped hand as they walked over to Murphy.

"You were right, Miguel. This is going to be one fascinating case by the looks of it," Murphy said.

Angus took in the greenish brown skeletal remains that lay curled into a fetal position inside the barrel and watched as the forensics team transported it onto a PVC sheet. Murphy told them to be careful and preserve whatever fluid was left inside the drum.

"Why is it so moist and slimy?" Angus asked. "It looks like something from a sci-fi movie."

"It's remarkable, isn't it? Nearly perfectly preserved like a giant pickle in a jar," Murphy answered.

"That's disgusting," Miguel commented.

"It's decomposition fluids combined with condensation from being sealed inside the steel keg."

"Any first observations?" asked Angus.

"You mean besides that it looks like an alien." She laughed then continued. "I can't be sure without proper testing, but I can tell you she's been in here a really long time."

"How long, if you had to hazard a guess," Angus asked.

Murphy scanned her eyes over the badly decomposed body.

"Taking the degree of preservation from being sealed inside the steel keg into consideration, I'd say anywhere between ten and fifteen years. Might even be longer."

Angus took a long pause then said, "Miguel, bring this Digby guy in for questioning. We can't rule him out until his story checks out."

Miguel gave a mock salute in agreement and left to do as he was instructed.

But less than a minute later, he came running around the house toward them.

"He's gone, Sheriff! Digby ran."

CHAPTER TWELVE

Angus scanned the small crowd that had already gathered in front of the house on Birch Lane while his mind raced with questions.

"Why would the guy run unless he had something to hide?" he muttered.

"Guilty people run, Sheriff," Miguel said.

Miguel was right, Angus thought. He had seen something hidden behind the man's earlier far-too-eager-to-help demeanor.

"Send out a few men," he instructed Miguel. "He couldn't have gone far. Besides, a guy dressed like that will stand out like a sore thumb in this town. With cowboy boots like those he's bound to get noticed quickly."

"On it, Sheriff."

Before long, Miguel had dispatched a small team of deputies and put out a description of the man.

"Bring Digby into the office when you find him, Miguel. I'll meet you there."

As the men parted ways, Angus met Murphy as she was preparing to leave.

"I should have asked you this before but how sure are you the body's female?" Angus asked.

Murphy pulled back the zipper on the body bag that lay on the gurney behind her, exposed the curled up corpse's head, and pointed out the barely there strands of hair.

"For one, these are definite remains of long hair, although, one can't always use that as a determining factor these days. But, if you also take into consideration the petite frame and narrow hips, it's definitely female." She closed up the bag and turned to face a worried-looking Angus. "I'll get cracking on our Jane Doe right away, Angus. I know this one's going to get a lot of attention."

"It already has, Doc," he said as he pointed his chin toward the small crowd before he thanked Murphy and left.

BY THE TIME Angus made it back to the office, he had already received a call from Miguel that Mr. Digby had been found hiding in his rental car down by the beach. Tammy met Angus as he walked in.

"Morning, Sheriff. This case has caused quite the stir this morning. The phone hasn't stopped ringing."

"I know. You're going to need to be alert. We don't want to create panic so stick to the usual script for now, please."

"Will do. I've also got that information Miguel asked for." She picked up a folder from her desk and followed Angus into his office.

"The airline confirmed his arrival this morning as well as one flight about a month ago. Nothing prior to that."

"Can you check with the other airlines?"

"Already have. I'm just waiting for them to get back to me. I've taken the liberty of having them run the check for the past two years, just in case."

"Clever thinking, thanks. How about the holder of the deed to the house?"

"That might be a bit harder to track down. The clerk's office has no record of the deed at all."

Angus frowned.

"That's impossible. I'm no expert on property law but as far as I know they have to hold a copy of the deed."

"I had them check twice, Sheriff. There's no record of it at all."

She handed the folder to Angus.

"I'll let you know when the airlines get back to me. Anything else I can do for you?"

"Thanks, Tammy, great work. Just keep the Weyport Herald at bay for now and let's keep a lid on things as much as possible, okay?"

"10-4, Sheriff."

As Tammy left his office, Miguel and two deputies escorted a rather nervous looking Mr. Digby to one of the interrogation rooms.

"He's already insisting on waiting for his lawyer, Sheriff," Miguel said as he popped his head around the door.

"So, he already made a call?"

Miguel nodded.

"Did you manage to get anything else out of him?"

"Nothing. He's as tight as a fresh clam shell."

From his office, Angus watched Digby through the window that looked into the interrogation room.

"He's fidgeting a lot for a man who's not guilty. Let's get him some coffee or a soda or something to loosen him up a bit. We're going to have to act quickly before his lawyer gets here."

A minute later, Angus gathered the folder Tammy had given him as well as a Styrofoam cup of coffee, shot up a prayer that that man would open up, and walked into the interrogation room.

He placed it on the table in front of Digby and sat down opposite him while Miguel stood against the wall next to him.

"Mr. Digby, I'm Sheriff Reid."

Digby shuffled uncomfortably in his seat.

"I'm not saying a word without my lawyer present," he said.

"You're not under arrest, Mr. Digby. We just need to

ask you a few questions. It's just to help us rule you out," Angus said.

"Rule me out? Of course, I'm *ruled* out. I have nothing to do with this, nothing," Digby said, the veins in his temples pulsing harder with each word.

"Then help us find out who does."

Digby didn't comment and Angus decided to change tactics.

"You must be exhausted. I heard you spent the night stranded at the airport," Angus continued gently. "The office coffee isn't too bad but if you prefer something else, we can run across to the diner to get you something."

Digby shook his head and accepted the cup of coffee.

"This is fine, thanks," he said, seeming to relax a bit.

"Why did you run, Mr. Digby?"

Digby set the coffee down.

"Wouldn't you? I mean, finding a body buried under your house does not happen every day, you know. I know how these things work."

"So, it's your house and you're the registered owner?"

Digby shifted in his chair, his fingers fiddling with the brim of his white cowboy hat which was on the table in front of him.

Angus waited for him to answer, but he didn't.

"We're just trying to make sense of this, Mr. Digby. We'll find out sooner or later anyway."

Digby pushed the coffee aside.

"If I'm not under arrest for anything, I'd like to go

please."

"Unfortunately, it doesn't quite work like that, Mr. Digby."

He gently leaned in across the table.

"I told you, Sheriff, I have nothing to do with that thing found under the house. I am as shocked about this as you are. You cannot keep me here against my will. I have a reputation to uphold, and I know my rights." He folded his arms across his chest.

Angus paused then shifted gears again.

"I understand you're a writer. Anything I might have read?" Angus asked.

A slight glimmer of pride flickered in Digby's eyes.

"I guess if you read crime novels you might have."

"Crime novels, huh? It makes sense why you ran then. Except, in the real world, we don't go around arresting people without sufficient evidence. But, perhaps we can help each other out, since I'm sure you are as eager as we are to get this over with. And who knows, this might turn into the inspiration for your next novel."

Digby's chin lifted, his shoulders pulled back, and his eyes lit up as if ideas for a plot had already started taking shape. Clearly liking the notion, he picked up the cup of coffee again and took a sip, gesturing that he was open to answering more questions.

Angus seized the opportunity.

"Why don't you start by telling me who the registered owner of the house on Birch Lane is?" Angus tried again.

CHAPTER THIRTEEN

Digby paused, his eyes nervously darting back and forth between Angus and Miguel.

"I can't," he said.

"You can't?" Angus asked incredulously.

"Yes, I can't. I'm not sure," Digby almost whispered the words.

Angus looked at him with confusion, but it was Miguel who interjected, annoyance dripping from his voice.

"How are you not sure, Mr. Digby? The construction workers confirmed they were working under your commission. You put down a substantial deposit toward the renovations. Why do that if the property isn't yours? Are you the owner of 16 Birch Lane or not?"

Miguel's impatient tone seemed to trigger something inside Digby that instantly shut him down.

"Like I said, Sheriff, if I am not under arrest I'd like to leave. You can submit any questions you have for me via my lawyer when he gets here."

Angus leaned back in his chair contemplating his next best approach when Tammy knocked on the door and popped her head inside.

"Sheriff, a word, if you can?" she whispered and waited for him to join her outside the room.

"Sorry to interrupt, but the guy's lawyer just called with strict instructions not to question his client until he gets here. He's just boarded a flight from Boston."

The news left Angus frustrated as he returned to the interrogation room and faced Digby.

"We can't force you to cooperate, Mr. Digby, not yet anyway. But I would strongly advise that you don't leave town."

The words had barely been spoken when Digby was up and on his feet, settling his cowboy hat back in place on his head.

Angus squared in front of him.

"Since you know how these things work, I suppose I also don't need to remind you that the house is a crime scene, so it goes without saying that any further renovation is off limits, Mr. Digby. I suggest you find yourself a place to stay until we clear you."

Digby's eyes expressed his displeasure before he turned and left without saying another word.

When only Angus and Miguel were alone in the room, Miguel rambled off an apology.

"I'm sorry. I don't know what came over me. I just had it with this guy playing games and taking us for fools. He clearly knows more than he's letting on."

Angus turned to face his deputy.

"In this game, Miguel, patience is your biggest virtue. All criminals trip up sooner or later."

"It won't happen again."

Angus squeezed his shoulder.

"Apology accepted. Besides, I don't think this guy is our murderer anyway."

"How do you figure that? He as much as admitted that it was his house. First by slipping up and then by avoiding the question. And why lawyer up so quickly if he is innocent? The guy's got guilt written all over his face."

Angus perched himself on the edge of the table.

"He knows something, all right, but he doesn't have an arrogant bone in his body. Most killers have an ego, a kind of *you'll never catch me* arrogance, but not this guy. Digby has no backbone and he's too concerned with his appearance and what people might think of him. That's why he lawyered up so quickly. That white hat of his doesn't have a spec of dirt on it. It's all for show, an image he tries to put out to the world - Rowley Digby, crime fiction writer. Trust me, this isn't our guy. Besides, why would he commission a renovation that involves pulling up the foundations if he knew he had hidden a body underneath? However, I do believe he does know something, I'll give you that, so let's get digging into who he is, okay? We have to grab what we can get our hands on before his lawyer shuts everything down, if he hasn't already. Look into his financial records and see if you can find out if the guy has any mortgages or loans. Check with Tammy if she's heard back from the airlines."

"On it, Sheriff," Miguel said as he spun around and set off toward his desk, new vigor in his step.

And as Angus sat down behind his own desk, he knew exactly where to take his investigation next. It was an angle with which he was far too familiar.

His fingers danced across his keyboard, and it wasn't long before his screen filled up with a list of women's names who had been reported missing over the last fifteen years.

CHAPTER FOURTEEN

Patty's eyes were fixed on the face of the grandfather clock. It had just chimed for two fifteen and she pushed her bowl of salad aside. She had no appetite for her lunch today. Neither had she eaten breakfast. She'd never been someone who could eat when her stomach was in knots.

She cleared the salad away, dropping all the contents into her compost container before she went into the living room and once again took up a position in front of the window. Daniel hadn't come home the night before and unrest had settled deep inside her stomach. It wasn't like him to not come home. No matter how many times they had disagreed in the past, he would always come home.

Patty stared out across the front lawn where remnants of the storm lay scattered across the lush green grass. She had lived in Weyport nearly all her life and she had never seen a storm quite this vicious come through. It was as if the heavens had poured out its wrath upon them.

She stood planted in front of the window, arms folded across each other as she anxiously rolled each shiny white pearl around her neck between her fingers. She had spent most of the night praying. Partly because she couldn't sleep but mostly out of fear for Daniel being out in the storm somewhere.

In his haste Daniel had left his cell behind so she had called Bill's wife, Belinda, at the first sign of light, hoping that Bill might have seen Daniel the night before. It was a long shot, she knew, but it wasn't as if Daniel had any friends in town and Belinda had been her closest friend since college. But neither had seen or heard from him since the run-in at the mayor's office. When she checked with Tammy at the sheriff's office if any car accidents had been reported, she was told that many of the roads were closed due to downed trees but that Tammy would let her know if she heard anything.

In the background, Patty had left the radio on, turning the volume up each time reports about damage the storm had caused were announced. There were several reports of fallen trees and streets that were flooded near the river, but no accidents.

She dropped the lace curtain back in place and, for the third time that day, walked into the guest room to check if perhaps Daniel had somehow slunk in. But everything was exactly as it had been when he left the night before.

Seeing the room empty again brought his callous words back to mind, pushing a fresh pang of hurt to her heart. Why would he say those horrible things about her? She had never wished him harm or done anything to make him believe she would be better off without him. On the contrary, she had loved him as best she could after his infidelity. She had chosen to forgive him, asked God to heal her heart, and had asked God to help her love him again. It hadn't been an easy eighteen years and the void between them had certainly increased but wishing him dead had never entered her mind or in her heart. That went against everything she believed as a Christ follower.

Perhaps he harbored guilt or maybe he needed more proof of her forgiveness. Or perhaps he was the one who had stopped loving her a long time ago.

She slammed the guest bedroom door shut behind her and with it, the painful memories that threatened to devour her once again.

"Not today, Satan!" she shouted into the hallway and darted to her purse and car keys that were on the side table in the foyer.

"You want proof, Daniel Richardson? I'll give you proof you old fool!" she said as she snatched up her keys and purse and hurried out of the house toward her car.

Leaves and sticks that had broken off the overhead tree lay thick across her front windshield and the hood of the car. But she had a sudden fire in her belly that blasted bolts of energy through her sixty-seven-year-old body, and she wiped them off with a few quick strokes.

Once behind the wheel, she backed out of the drive and took off in the same direction she had watched Daniel go the night before. She leaned over her steering wheel to look up at the blue sky. It couldn't have been a better day, not an angry cloud left in sight, as if the storm had never even happened.

If only the storm in her heart would clear away as quickly, she thought.

She drove slowly through the neighborhood. Empty trashcans that had been blown into the street lay toppled over on the sidewalks and the neighborhood was a flurry of activity as people cleaned away broken branches and leaves.

She took the route she assumed Daniel would have taken if he had gone to the cigar bar he sometimes stopped at on the way home after a hard day's work. Her sights trailed the streets in search of his red car. When she eventually reached the bar, she pulled into the small parking area next to it. Apart from one vehicle that carried the branding of a local cleaning company, the rest of the parking lot was entirely empty. Not wasting any time, she backed out and decided to zigzag through the center of town. But Daniel's flashy little red BMW was nowhere to be seen.

Out of ideas, she pulled over to the side of the road, her fingers nervously tapping the steering wheel as she contemplated what to do next. Doubt took root nearly instantly. Perhaps Daniel left town. Perhaps he didn't want to be found.

A swell of tears threatened behind her eyes. It would be easy to just give up and go home, carry on about her day, keep herself busy so she wouldn't have time to think about the hole he had left all those years ago. Or about the fresh scars he had made the night before. But something was holding her back. Something stopped her from turning her car around and locking her feelings up inside. She shut her eyes for a brief moment, directed her spirit heavenward, and waited.

What do I do, Lord? She prayed in silence. Her prayerful pause continued for a few minutes hearing nothing back from the One who had sustained her during her years of loneliness. Nearly giving up hope, she slowly opened her eyes. In the nearby window of the bank, her eyes caught the large poster that was prominently displayed .

Bill Baxter's smug face stared back at her from where he proudly stood in front of a mockup of the proposed residential layout of his lakeside development.

Her heart skipped a beat and she knew instantly the Holy Spirit had directed her to this spot, to see this poster, and to direct her next steps.

If there was one thing Patty knew about her husband, then it was that he was as stubborn as they came.

Daniel Richardson had only ever had one mission in

life and that was to protect his grandfather's legacy with everything he possessed inside. He was used to getting his way and that stubborn arrogance had made him do a great many stupid things to prove just how serious he was when it came to protecting his family name.

And stupid took on an entirely new meaning if Daniel had determined that protecting his legacy extended to the only thing standing in the way of Bill Baxter. Especially if Bill stood to profit from something Daniel felt the man didn't deserve.

CHAPTER FIFTEEN

Patty revved her car through the downtown Weyport streets to where she eventually turned toward the lake.

As was the case everywhere else, the road was hard to navigate, and she had to slow to a crawl in several places. Large branches lay strewn across the road, and she carefully maneuvered around them. Patty's patience wore thin as she drove through the heavily forested area. On several occasions, she found herself pulling her shoulders to her ears as she heard a branch scratch away at her car's body paint.

WHEN SHE EVENTUALLY REACHED THE turnoff to the lake, she stopped at the top of the sandy road and took in the multiple water-filled potholes that stood between her and, hopefully, Daniel. She puffed a mouthful of air out between her lips and visually plotted the best route. Given that her car wasn't equipped to handle rough terrain, there was little she could do to circumvent the holes and chose to leave it up to God to help her through.

The unstable sand gave way beneath her wheels and she decided to speed up, remembering a piece of advice she had once heard. The last thing she wanted was to be stuck in the sand. Thankfully, her Japanese-made vehicle was smaller and lighter than most. It bounced over the road, sending her out of her seat a few times but she kept going, knowing if she stopped she might not be able to get her car going again.

To her right, was a sight to behold. Tall trees overlooked the lake at the edge of the expansive stretch of land Bill was proposing to develop. As soon as her gaze slid to the end of the road where Daniel's land crossed directly between the lake and Bill's intended homes, she realized why Bill needed the Richardson land.

Her momentary lack of focus cost her as a tire hit a deep puddle and the car jerked to an abrupt halt, sending Patty toward the dashboard. Her chest hurt where the seat belt restrained her and she took a moment to get her breath back.

"Pay attention, Patty," she reprimanded herself before she pushed her foot down on the accelerator.

The engine revved loudly as sand kicked up underneath her car, indicating she'd gotten the car stuck, the very thing she'd been trying to avoid. "Just great!" she exclaimed.

She turned the car off, deciding she'd walk the last stretch of the road in hopes of finding Daniel. She assumed he had hit the same hindrances and had probably been waiting it out in his car until a fisherman or bird watcher came along.

When she stepped out of her car, she sank nearly knee-deep in the soft, wet sand. Patty grabbed onto the car door to keep her balance. As she attempted to pull herself out of the waterlogged hole, she lost a shoe in the process. She wriggled and wrestled against the sand that didn't want to let go, as if it had a mind of its own. Using the steering wheel, Patty attempted to pull herself back into the car, nearly losing her balance. She fought harder.

Beneath the cold sand her foot hit something hard and she yelled out in pain. *Picnic-goers leave their glass bottles everywhere!* she thought in anger, biting down on her bottom lip as the pain shot through her foot and up her leg.

She fell back into the car and landed in a half seated position on the floor. The door frame provided the support she needed to take the weight off her legs, and she freed her feet from the sandy trap. Out of breath, she managed to pull herself back into the seat of the car and looked down at her feet to see a nasty gash that ran across the side of one of her feet. Droplets of blood could be seen in the puddle and now on the floor of her car. The sight caused her face to scrunch up and she leaned across to the glovebox where she kept a box of Kleenex. When she had stopped the bleeding, she wrapped her foot in the silk neckerchief she had thankfully tied around her neck that morning.

Feeling defeated she stared down at the puddle of water outside her door, studying the size of it. She would have to climb out the other side, she realized and, as stealthily as her body allowed her, soon found herself exiting her car from the passenger side.

Now on solid ground, she walked around the car and carefully approached the area that had tried to swallow her legs and feet. Whatever was down there hadn't slashed her tire but she might not escape it a second time if she left it there. She crouched down next to the puddle and allowed her hands to carefully search for the object, slowly inching her way toward the spot. When her fingers found it, she realized that the object wasn't the broken bottle she had expected to find.

Puzzled, she worked to remove whatever was buried beneath the sand and removed a metal box slightly larger than a shoebox from the ground and dropped it on the sand next to her. She stared at the dark green container that resembled the ones used by the military. It seemed to be several decades old and Patty was surprised at how well it had held together even with it being rusted in several places. A relatively modern silver padlock dangled from the front of the box. This too showed some corrosion but not enough for it to be opened without the key.

Above her head, a flock of herring gulls squawked noisily as they headed toward the lake, reminding her why she was there. She reached back into the puddle to retrieve her missing shoe and shut the metal box inside the trunk of her car. For now, whatever was locked away inside the box would have to wait.

If there was a chance Daniel got stuck in the sand like she did, she'd have to hurry to find him before the sun went down.

CHAPTER SIXTEEN

P atty had nearly reached the end of the road when she spotted Daniel's little red car parked at the edge of his family's land. She stopped, cupped her hand over her eyes to block the sun from her vision, and called out.

"Daniel!" She listened as her voice echoed across the open land and lake.

She called a second time as she hurriedly made her way across the sandy terrain toward his car. The sand had found its way in between her silk wrapping and the gash on the side of her foot, and the tiny grains chafed across the wound. It stung but she kept going.

She moved as fast as she could through the sand, the aches in her knees reminding her that she wasn't as fit as she used to be. Every few paces she glanced up at the car, her eyes searching for Daniel, expecting the worst. He would have been out there all night and, unlike her,

Daniel refused even the smallest medical check-up and wasn't in the kind of shape she was. When she got to his vehicle, she saw that his driver's side door was opened wide, and her heart bolted into her throat.

Blood was on the seat and down along the side of the door. Suddenly her legs didn't want to cooperate, and she stood there staring for the briefest of moments. Fear sat shallow in the pit of her stomach.

"Daniel?" she gently called out again, her voice near panic.

Silence.

Her chest filled with dread. Her mind conjured images of finding his dead body somewhere next to the car followed by thoughts of Bill doing unspeakable harm. He was a ruthless man who had sold his soul to mammon a long time ago. Without Daniel's land, he stood to lose far more money than his greed would allow. And if what Belinda had told her was true, Bill's business wasn't doing as well as he made everyone believe. That was certainly enough cause to want to bully his way into getting what he wanted.

After Patty walked around the car and didn't find Daniel, she yanked open the trunk.

But this too was empty. There was no sight or sound of Daniel anywhere.

She squinted her eyes toward the lake then turned around to take in the area where the edge of the forest met the lake. She was certain she had seen something move.

Perhaps a deer, she thought, and turned her attention back to the car.

But moments later, a dull thumping sound drifted in the breeze toward her, and she stopped to look back at a spot between the trees. She listened. There it was again, a faint but definite wood knocking.

"Daniel!" she yelled, instinctively knowing it was him. "I'm coming, hang on!"

The knocking stopped, a clear sign to her that it was him. She set off toward the trees, following the blotches of dark red sand where they guided her way toward the forest, like a trail of breadcrumbs from her favorite childhood fairytale. At least Daniel was alive. That much she now knew. What she did not know was what she'd find when she got to him or how they were going to get home.

But at least he was alive.

AS SHE APPROACHED the tree line, Daniel's slumped-over body came into view. He sat leaning up against the trunk of a large tree, his head dropped forward onto his chest.

"Daniel, I'm here," she called out when she was about ten yards away from him.

Daniel didn't answer.

Pain shot into her foot with each step as she quickly but carefully traversed the broken branches that covered nearly every inch of the ground under the trees. When she finally got to him, she saw what had caused Daniel to bleed all over the car and sand.

An audible gasp left her throat as she took it all in.

"Oh, Daniel!" she cried out when she saw the piece of wood lodged in his side.

"It's okay, I'm here now," she tried to assure him.

But in truth, her insides were trembling while her mind frantically tried to make sense of it all.

She gently lifted Daniel's chin to find his eyes closed.

"Daniel, stay with me, you have to stay awake, you hear me?"

He moaned and she took her cardigan off and covered his wet, shivering body. Her hands went to where the thin tree branch had pierced through his shirt and into his side. Around it, his clothes were drenched in blood.

When she pulled back at the fabric trying to get a better look, Daniel moaned in pain.

"It's bad, " she said, squeamish at the sight of it. "You've lost a lot of blood. I know you're probably not going to like me saying this, but we have to get you to the hospital."

He blinked slowly in agreement, surprising her with how quickly he agreed. Normally he'd fight her and eventually she'd give in. But not now, a sign that he was fully aware that he'd run out of options.

Patty tried to stay calm, but her mind was in a state of panic. They were in the middle of nowhere with her car stuck in the sand half a mile away, no cell service, and far too far for him in the condition he was in.

She pushed herself up off the ground and peered over the lake in search of a boat or anyone who could help.

But the lake was calm and devoid of any human activity.

"Does your car work?" she asked.

He shook his head ever so slightly.

"How long have you been here like this? All night?"

He blinked and nodded slowly.

"My car is stuck in a giant pothole up the road. I'm going to have to go at it by foot and try to find help. You stay here, okay? I'll be back as soon as I can."

Daniel's mouth curled into a half smile and raised one eyebrow as if to say where else would I go?

"Whatever, you old fool," she said as she smiled back then gave him a gentle kiss on his forehead.

Without wasting another minute, she ran off toward the lake, praying that God would send help.

As she ran, she tried to make sense of the situation but the farther she went, the more questions arose. Why was Daniel there, and how was it possible that a branch impaled him when he had clearly been inside his car based on how much blood had been on the steering wheel, seat, and door? Even with the strong winds of the storm, it simply didn't make sense.

Unless it wasn't caused by the storm.

CHAPTER SEVENTEEN

Angus stood staring at the evidence board they had put up in the small conference room, waiting for his investigating team to gather around for a feedback meeting. His eyes studied the photo of Digby. He was their only suspect and a weak one at that.

He glanced at his watch. They had been at it all day and knew nothing more than they had five hours ago.

Miguel, Tammy, and one other deputy who had been assisting in gathering information filed in one by one and sat down at the table.

He turned to face them, wasting no time on small talk.

"Please tell me at least one of you has something concrete to go on."

Miguel shook his head.

"There's nothing on this Digby character. His financials are squeaky clean. No large sums or any irregular payments going in or out of his bank accounts. A few phone calls a day, mostly to his wife, Vanessa. He's not as famous as he'd like us to believe either. Earns just enough to cover the one mortgage they have, a modest house in one of Nashville's average neighborhoods. He's nothing special and there's not much else to say about the guy," Miguel finished.

"The house in Nashville, is it his?" Angus asked.

"Yes, and as far as I'm able to see, the only one he owns."

"What about his wife, Vanessa?"

"She's co-owner of their Nashville house and the owner of a small artisan cake shop."

Angus dropped his head to his chest and settled his hands on his hips before he turned his attention to Tammy.

"Anything from the airlines?"

"Actually, yes. The guy lied. He's been here more than the two times he said he was. According to the logs, he's been here half a dozen times before today, spanning the past two years. Stays for three or four days then flies back out again. The airlines' records don't go back any earlier."

Miguel's interest was piqued.

"I knew he was lying," he said.

"The question is, why is he lying? And what about his claim that he inherited the house from his uncle?" Angus looked at Tammy.

"Also, a lie," she answered. "I called in a favor from a

friend of mine at the county's office and he said there is definitely no deed to this property. Not six months ago and not now. He even checked the archives for me."

"It's not possible," Angus said. "What about utility services to the house, electricity, water? There has to be a record of someone owning this house."

"The power company is looking into this but as far as they're aware, they've never charged any bills to the house, and they have no record of ever receiving instructions to connect electricity or gas to the property. Not even a telephone line or internet. No payments either."

"So, no paper trail whatsoever," Miguel commented.

"Whoever's been living there has been living for free? How is that even possible in today's day and age?" Angus asked.

He turned to face the evidence board again, his back to his team. Something about this case teased at his emotions, made him angry and sad at the same time. Did the dead woman's family just turn their backs on her? At what point did they stop looking for her? He silently vowed to never give up on his brother like his mother did. He would keep searching until he found him, dead or alive.

Miguel spoke behind him, bringing his thoughts back to the present.

"I'll look into Digby's family. See if he even had an uncle."

Angus turned to face him, nodded, and changed directions.

"Let's shift the focus to our Jane Doe for a minute. I've pulled a list of names of all the women reported missing over the last fifteen years. Most cases have been closed as being either deceased or found. The remaining ones are cold cases, mostly young kids who clearly don't match our Jane Doe."

"So, we're back to square one," Miguel said.

"Not necessarily. Perhaps the reports weren't filed in this county. Our Jane Doe could have been killed somewhere else and her body buried here."

"I'll expand the search to neighboring counties," Tammy volunteered.

"Perfect, let's start there and widen the search. Miguel, take a closer look into Digby's background. Also, see what you can find on his wife. Find out what her maiden name was. Cross-reference that to mortgages. This guy is hiding something or someone. For all we know, he's protecting his wife. Tammy, I want that deed. There *has* to be one." Angus turned to the second deputy. "Go back to the house and check with the neighbors. Maybe they know something, kept mail, anything."

Angus started walking to the door and spoke over his shoulder, "I'm going to check in with Dr. Delaney. We need a name, her age, time of death, something. I want no stone unturned."

. . .

THE TEAM SPLIT up and Angus entered Dr. Murphy Delaney's office.

"I was just about to call you," Murphy said when he approached the body she was examining.

"You got something for me, Doc?"

"I hope so. I still need to do some tests, but upon a first examination, I can tell you she sustained a significant blow to the head. I can't say if it is what killed her, but it would certainly have knocked her out cold."

"You're saying there's a possibility that someone knocked her over the head and buried her alive?"

"It's possible, but I won't know for sure until I run all the tests. Considering the degree of decomposition, the tests are a lot more intricate, most of which I'll have to send to the FBI lab for testing."

"And that can take weeks," Angus sighed.

"All is not lost, Angus. I might not be able to point you to the murder weapon or cause of death yet, but I figured you could do more at this stage by knowing when she died. I focused most of my attention there. Albeit it's an approximate time of death, but at least it might narrow things down for you."

Angus perked up and Murphy continued.

"Initially, I had estimated her to have been dead for ten to fifteen years. Well, it turns out it's more like fifteen to twenty years. It's truly remarkable. If she had been buried in a plastic container or a coffin, or even just in the bare soil, it would have been an entirely different result.

But like I said this morning, the steel keg significantly slowed the decomposition."

"You're sure?" Angus asked.

"Fairly certain, yes. I'll be able to confirm it by tomorrow morning when my supporting tests run through their sequences. But wait, there's more," she said playfully. "I can also tell you that she must have been about thirty to thirty-five years old at the most. Her bone density correlates to the range expected for that of a female falling within that age group."

The good news drove a flurry of excitement through Angus and, without thinking, he grabbed Murphy by the shoulders and planted a fat kiss on her cheek.

"You're the best, Murphy, thank you!"

Instantly the space between them turned awkward.

Murphy blushed, her big brown eyes fixed to his mouth.

Angus froze, knowing she wanted more. He let go of her shoulders and took a few steps back, his hand combing through his hair as he looked down at the floor.

"I'm sorry, I shouldn't have done that. That was very unprofessional of me."

She smiled at him.

"Do you hear me complaining?"

Her comment caught him off guard and he was rendered speechless, knowing he could not provide the response he knew she was hoping for.

He cleared his throat. In another lifetime he would

have seized the opportunity and kissed her but something inside him had him pull away from her, shutting down the ability to feel that way about a woman again.

"Thanks Doc, I have to go," he rambled uncomfortably then turned and rushed out the door.

When he got into his car, he laid his head back and shut his eyes for a brief moment. He shouldn't have done that, shouldn't have taken her to all those breakfasts, and led her on. It wasn't fair. She deserved better, he told himself.

CHAPTER EIGHTEEN

The sun sat low on the horizon, casting its final golden rays across the silky smooth surface of the lake. Patty had searched all the fishing spots along the forest side of the lake in the hope of finding anyone who could help them. But there wasn't a single person in sight, not even a late afternoon owner walking his dog.

She hurried back to where she had left Daniel at the edge of the forest, angry with herself for wasting valuable time looking for help. What if she got back and Daniel was... she blocked the horrific thought. Keep him safe, Lord, she prayed instead. Send someone and show me what to do.

The cold wind sliced through her thin blouse, and she wondered if her cardigan was enough to keep Daniel warm. The thought of losing him provided a surge of energy to push harder through the thick foliage that lined the lake, her speed hindered by her swollen foot. She glanced back at the sun. It would be dark soon and if he were to survive another night, she would have to somehow get him into his car.

When she rounded the last trees, she leaned against a thick trunk to catch her breath to keep her legs from giving out beneath her. Patty caught sight of Daniel seated in the precise position as when she had left him. She pushed her exhausted body away from the trunk and ran the final few yards to him.

"Daniel, I'm back, I'm here," she panted.

He didn't stir.

"Daniel, can you hear me?"

Tremors pushed into her dainty hands as they went to his face. His skin felt ice cold and she snatched back her hands, cupping them under her chin. Her heart bounced wildly in her chest.

With trembling fingers, her hand went to the folds of his neck. When she couldn't feel his heartbeat, she wriggled her fingers deeper under the squishy flesh of his double chin and pushed down harder.

Daniel moaned softly.

"Oh, Daniel, you're alive," she nearly wept with joy and lifted his chin to find his gaze but his eyes were closed.

Shock rippled through her body once again as she noticed the ashen tone of his face.

"Okay, we need to get you out of the cold and into the car."

He moaned again.

"It's not up for debate, old man," she intentionally pushed a button she knew would annoy him, hoping it would encourage him to fight back.

As predicted, it stirred a reaction and Daniel frowned then slowly opened his eyes.

"That's it, use that anger to fight your way to the car. Come on, get up." Her arm curled around his torso to help him up.

Daniel screamed in agony as the shift in position tugged at his open wound.

She blurted out an apology knowing there was no way to avoid his discomfort. It took another four attempts and several guttural moans before she finally managed to lift him to his feet. Every muscle in her body ached but there was no time to wallow in self-pity.

Careful not to move the wooden spear, she draped one of his arms around her shoulders and tried to ignore the throbbing in her injured foot that increased with his added weight. Daniel was weak, and she had to do whatever she could to get him out of the cold.

When her energy waned and her body threatened to collapse, she prayed for superhuman strength. God must have heard her because she managed to get into a slow rhythm.

"Good, one foot in front of the other, old man. Let's go," she drilled Daniel into motion until step by baby step, the distance to the car grew shorter and shorter.

Darkness had fallen around them by the time she got Daniel onto the backseat of his little car, his body far too large to lay down all the way. She used his grandfather's coat to prop his head up and get him as comfortable as possible. But the broken branch in his side stuck out and kept hooking into the tan leather seats. At one stage, she contemplated pulling it out, but every time she pulled away the fabric of his shirt, fresh blood gushed out.

Panic increased with each passing moment as she watched him fade in and out of consciousness.

"Don't you dare die on me, Daniel Richardson! Do you hear me? You fight, like your grandfather taught you to."

Daniel wasn't responding.

Her bloodstained fists hammered on his chest as tears overtook her panic. She'd spent more than forty-five years of her life with this man by her side—through hardships most couples don't have to endure. She hadn't come all this way to let it slip through her fingers. Living on her own without him wasn't an option. Not like this. They had unfinished business between them, amends to make.

"Daniel, I won't let you leave me behind. Are you listening to me? You're all I have left in this life; don't die on me, not like this."

Sadness spilled from her as if he had already died and when she caught her breath, she stepped back and stood outside the car. The wind was icy cold against her flushed cheeks, and she drew in a sharp breath, wiping the wetness from her face. She stared at the car, hugged herself in an attempt to warm up, and inhaled a new round of determination.

"You're not going to get your way with me, red car, you hear me?" She told it off as if it were human. "Your driver is dying in the back so do whatever you need to do to work and get us to the hospital, right now!"

She climbed in behind the wood-trim steering wheel, took a deep breath, and willed the car to start.

"Please start, please start," she whispered, her eyes pinched closed as she turned the key in the ignition.

Perhaps it was her scolding tone, or most likely, a divine hand, but the engine whirred into action on the first turn.

She yelled out in elation, a large grin on her face.

"We're getting out of here, Daniel, sit tight! I'll have you to the hospital before you know it."

Her foot pressed down on the pedal, and she heard the wheels spinning in the sand.

"No, no, no!" she yelled out. "You behave now, you stupid little car, behave!"

The car was stuck in the sand and no matter how much she yelled at it as if it were human, it didn't budge.

A quick glance at Daniel behind her told her she couldn't give up and quitting wasn't in her genes. She jumped out and assessed what she was up against, contemplating how to get the car unstuck. The car's front wheel was nearly halfway submerged into the wet sand and she knelt down and started digging out the sand around it, fueled by sheer will and stubbornness to not let the sand win. When she had dug out the wheel, she reached back into the car and took Daniel's coat out from under his head. Laying it down on the sand in front of the wheel, she wriggled the fabric beneath the tire as best she could, scooping out sand along the way to weigh down the sides of the coat.

Satisfied it would do the trick, she got back into the car and put it into gear, saying a prayer. The tire slid ever so slightly then gained traction, pushing the car forward, skidding over his grandfather's coat until the little red car was free from the sandy mire.

CHAPTER NINETEEN

B ill Baxter nervously paced his office floor. His wife, Belinda, had just called with the news that Daniel was in hospital and that his condition was severe.

"Did you hear what I said, Bill?" Belinda had asked when he didn't respond to the news.

"I heard you. How bad is it?"

"Patty says it's really bad. He lost a lot of blood and, according to the doctors, it's touch and go at the moment."

"Nothing we can do then is there? Just let me know if you hear anything else, okay?" Bill said before he ended the call.

UNEASE TUGGED at the back of his mind and he leaned forward over his desk. It wasn't supposed to go like this. Stupid old fool. What was he thinking?

A thought far worse entered Bill's mind. If Daniel survived and started talking things could go horribly wrong for Baxter Enterprises. He could lose everything.

He turned and stared at the lake project's renderings on his wall. Why did Daniel have to be so stubborn? If only he hadn't fought him on it, gotten physical with him, then none of this would have happened. Bill knew he should not have gone back to the land after the team's search turned up empty. He should have just left it alone, waited until dark. But then Daniel showed up there in the middle of the day which was suspicious. He couldn't have avoided an altercation with Daniel even if he wanted to.

Bill played back the events of the day before. He knew they would eventually cross swords over that land but not like this. Nothing good could come from this.

Bill wondered who stood to inherit the land if Daniel died, as his reflections of the previous day turned toward greed. If Patty were sole heir to the Richardson land, it would be a slam-dunk thanks to her friendship with Belinda. However, if out of spite Daniel ceded it to some random conservation company that wanted to protect the surrounding wildlife, he wouldn't stand a chance moving ahead with the project.

Unless he discovered something far more valuable in the land than what met the eye. A smile broke across his face. Once Daniel was out of the picture he'd go back with the right equipment and make sure he found what Daniel was keeping secret on that piece of land.

His thoughts took an ominous turn. What if someone had seen him with Daniel the day before? He couldn't afford to have any witnesses. If Daniel survived, it would be game over. He'd surely tell everyone how he got hurt even though he knew it was an accident.

Bill's finger pressed the call button on his desk phone for his assistant.

"Get me an update on Daniel Richardson," Bill said forcefully.

"Yes, Sir," she replied.

Bill slumped into his chair, his eyes fixed on the phone as he waited, impatience tugging at his insides. After what seemed like way too long, his assistant popped her head around his door.

"Mr. Richardson's condition is critical, Mr. Baxter. He's still in the ICU. Mrs. Richardson says he's not regained consciousness since they got to the hospital last night."

Bill's fingertips tapped the desk.

"Do they know what happened?"

"She didn't go into any detail, Sir. She just said she found him with a stick piercing his side and that he had lost a lot of blood."

Having heard enough he waved for her to leave and pushed his concerns aside. Daniel's injury could have just as well been caused by the storm. The entire town was covered in debris from the storm. With any luck, Daniel would not live another day to tell his sordid tale and then there would be nothing standing in the way of Bill's dreams.

THE LIST of names and faces rolled across his computer screen as Angus worked his way through the few dozen missing person cases that were reported during his newly established timeline. He found himself more on edge than usual this morning, a familiar feeling he recognized whenever he went over cold cases. He'd never get used to it, he thought. Seeing their faces, happy, smiling, and unaware that their lives would be irrevocably changed forever. He paused scrolling and reached into his back pocket to retrieve his wallet. From behind one of the leather sleeves, he pulled out a small photo of him and his brother. It had been a while since he looked at it but something about this case scratched open old wounds.

The photo had been taken when they were still living in Scotland, standing on a cliff, the ocean in the background. It was one of the last pictures they had taken together. His brother was happy, smiling, and had his long, lean arm protectively draped around Angus' shoulder. Logan had always been the responsible one, keeping him from getting into trouble with their father. Angus rubbed his thumb over his brother's face, his mind momentarily lost in the memory of that day. When it brought too much emotion to the surface, he tucked the photo back inside the sleeve and tossed his wallet inside the top drawer of his desk.

He turned his attention back to the cold cases on his screen. None of them fit the age of their Jane Doe. It was as if she were a ghost, lost and forgotten in time—or erased.

The computer mouse under his hand clicked away at the files, and fear of not finding the truth teased at the back of his mind. It made him angry, feeling so helpless. He pushed the mouse to one side.

"You okay?" Miguel asked, walking into the office.

Angus leaned back in his chair.

"I will be once we close this case."

"Well, maybe that day is today," Miguel said under a wide grin. "I think I might have found something. It might be nothing but at this stage I'm not leaving anything to chance."

Angus sat up in his chair as he waited for Miguel to continue.

"I've been digging up everything I could get my hands on about this Digby guy. Surprise, surprise, there is no uncle, not on his side, nor his wife's. But, what I did find were adoption papers." He spread open the case file in front of Angus. "The Digbys adopted a child, a boy, about sixteen years ago. The adoption records were sealed. But there's something about this I just can't shake. According to the agency, the now retired caseworker says she clearly remembers this couple. She even held onto the original case file and says it's always puzzled her that after never wanting children, these two suddenly filed for adoption. And, for a one-year-old no less." Miguel dropped the caseworker's file on the desk and pointed to a picture of the boy. "The Digbys told her the boy was Vanessa's sister's child and that she wasn't able to take care of him. But the sister was never present to sign over her child's adoption. The caseworker said the Digbys made a substantial donation to the agency which, at the time, she accepted but apparently she has regretted doing so ever since. I'm still trying to figure out where the donation came from considering Rowley's average finances and all."

Angus frowned.

"This caseworker, she never thought to check if the kid might have been kidnapped? What's wrong with this world?"

"I know, right? Money does weird things to people. It erases all morals of even the most honest of people. Anyway, I'm going to look into the boy. If they did kidnap him then there's a good chance our Jane Doe might be his mother. That would help explain her body in the foundations of the Digby's house."

"Except we have no proof that the house does in fact belong to either Digby or that our Jane Doe is in any way connected to either of them."

"My gut tells me there is a connection there, Sheriff, and rest assured, Tammy and I will not give up until we find the evidence to prove it."

CHAPTER TWENTY

Angus shuffled through the papers in the folder, flipping through the photos of the child who looked to be about a year and a half at the time. When he turned his attention to a photo of Rowley Digby and his wife, he lingered on it.

"Wait!" Angus exclaimed when he saw the woman's face. "I've seen her. I've seen this woman."

He tossed the folder onto his desk and snatched the computer mouse, his fingers scrolling back and forth on the wheel.

"You have?" Miguel asked as he moved around the desk to see what Angus was looking for.

Angus stopped on a grainy black and white picture of a woman.

"Look! It's her! It's the same woman."

His voice was full of excitement.

Miguel took the photo from the folder and held it up next to the computer to compare.

"You're right. It's the same woman. That is Vanessa Digby."

Angus and Miguel studied the case file on the screen in front of them.

"Look at the date. It says this case was filed sixteen years ago, Sheriff."

"And it's still unsolved. It even coincides with Murphy's time of death."

Miguel pointed his finger at the computer screen.

"Look at her name though," he said when he read the name of the missing woman on the screen. The missing woman was identified as Kim Kincaid.

"It must be a computer error," said Angus as he got up from his desk and walked out the door to find Tammy.

"Do we have access to physical copies of case files from sixteen years ago?" he asked her.

"If there was one it should be in the archives in the basement. Which one are you looking for?"

He hurried back to his desk, and she followed him, taking the case number that he jotted down on a piece of paper.

"Be back in a jiffy, Sheriff."

Angus sat back down behind his desk while Miguel continued to pore over the adoption information in the folder he had brought with him.

"There's no mention in here of a Kim Kincaid. Not

on the adoption papers or the marriage license, nothing. Yet, these two pictures are a near perfect match. It has to be Vanessa Digby." Miguel dropped the folder on the desk. "I smell a giant rat. Or perhaps I'm missing something."

"No, I think you're right. Something about this cold case is off. Great work, Miguel."

"Thanks I was beginning to think we were dealing with a ghost here."

Angus shook his head.

"Even ghosts have a story to tell, and by the looks of things, it seems this ghost is still very much alive."

"It still doesn't explain who our Jane Doe is. If Vanessa Digby and Kim Kincaid are the same person, then who was buried in the barrel? Is it possible they made a mistake with the name when they transferred the file onto the computer?" Miguel asked.

"It's always a possibility. But at least this information gave us the first glimmer of hope in cracking this case."

Just then, Tammy burst in through the door, a smile on her face and a folder in her hand that she handed over.

Angus thanked her and immediately started flipping through the cold case file. His index finger traced down the sheet of paper that outlined the case.

"And? Was it a mistake?"

At first Angus didn't speak. He took the original photo from the cold case folder and held it up against the photo in Miguel's folder.

"Yeah, it's definitely Vanessa Digby," Miguel confirmed over his shoulder.

"I agree, but it seems there was no mistake made with their names." Angus pointed to several places on the documentation in the cold case folder.

"Ok, so she changed her name for some reason," Miguel suggested. "People do that all the time. For one, she got married to Digby so naturally her last name would have changed."

Angus slammed both folders shut, yanked his jacket off the back of his chair, and grabbed his wallet and car keys from his drawer.

"Let's go, Miguel," he said.

"Where are we going?"

"We're going to pay Mrs. Digby a little visit."

"You mean we're going to Nashville."

Angus nodded and said, "I reckon since Mr. Digby is stuck here, it might give us the perfect opportunity to ask his wife a few questions. For all we know, Vanessa Digby is the one in the barrel and the woman behind door number one is an imposter, posing as her. Or we arrive and there is no Mrs. Digby at all. In either case, with or without his lawyer, Mr. Digby will have a lot to answer for."

On their way out, Angus instructed Tammy to have two deputies keep an eye on Digby's whereabouts and make sure he didn't leave town. Less than an hour later, he and Miguel arrived at the airport and caught the next flight to Nashville.

BY THE TIME they arrived at Digby's Nashville house, it was late afternoon. The neighborhood was quiet and average looking, something that surprised Angus since Digby was clearly set on keeping up appearances. They parked their rental car on the street opposite his house and paused to observe the house.

"Think he's lying about having a wife?" Miguel asked when the house appeared to be unoccupied.

"I think he knows more than he lets on."

Angus got out and started crossing the road, Miguel a few steps behind. Approaching the front door, they saw slight movement behind one of the curtains.

"Someone's home all right," Angus commented and rang the doorbell.

It took another ring before a female voice answered, her face only slightly visible through the small crack of the open door behind the safety chain.

"Can I help you, officers?"

"Mrs. Digby?" Angus inquired.

"Yes?"

"I'm Sheriff Angus Reid from Weyport County, Maine. I was wondering if we could ask you a few questions about the house you and your husband have in Weyport."

Her eyes widened.

"You need to speak to my husband, please, Sheriff. I have nothing to say on the matter." She tried closing the door.

"Ma'am, I just need to know if you used to go by the name Kim Kincaid."

The woman's eyes stretched even wider before she shut the door in their faces.

"I'm not answering any questions! My husband said not to say anything. You need to talk to our lawyer," she yelled through the door.

Angus took a few steps back then turned and walked toward the rental car.

"That's it? We're just going to leave? We didn't even get a chance to properly see her face."

"It's the same woman, Miguel," Angus said solemnly. "That's Vanessa Digby and judging by the shocked look in her eyes, I'd say she was once also named Kim Kincaid."

CHAPTER TWENTY-ONE

Patty stared at her husband's pale face and white hair that blended into the white pillow under his head. In all the years they had been married she had never seen him this ill and most definitely never in a hospital bed.

Her eyes traced the multitude of tubes and wires that ran from his arm, waist, and mouth to various machines, her eyes freezing when they landed on the luminous green line jumping rhythmically on the screen on the other side of the bed. The doctor had said his heart rate was stable but compared to the heart thumping inside her chest, it seemed far too slow to convince her that he was out of danger.

She looked down at his hand she hadn't let go of since they got there. It was much larger than hers, the skin around his fingertips cracked and calloused, showing clear signs of a man who wasn't scared of hard work. She should have shown him more appreciation and respect, her thoughts taking her to his accusations of just a few nights before. Her heart filled with regret as her head dropped forward and rested on her arms on the side of the bed, her hands still clutching his lifeless hand. She said a silent prayer and asked God to forgive her for not honoring her husband in the way he deserved. She had taken him for granted, assuming he would be around forever.

Her melancholic thoughts were interrupted by one of the night nurses.

"Mrs. Richardson, you should go home and get some rest. I'll call you if anything changes."

Patty sat up straight and shook her head.

"He needs me. He needs to know I'm here and that I haven't left his side."

The words sounded hollow, masked under a blanket of counterfeit courage.

"I'm sure he knows that already. Besides, the doctor said he might not regain consciousness for another few days. Your husband lost a significant amount of blood and his left kidney is fighting off a bad infection. There's nothing you can do for him right now except wait. I give you my word; I will phone you the moment he wakes up." The nurse gently placed her hand on Patty's back. "Go home and get some rest. Your husband will need you more once he wakes up."

Patty's eyes darted between Daniel's face and the nurse's reassuring smile. She was exhausted and hadn't changed out of the bloodied clothes since they got there. Her foot, although clean and stitched up, could do with being propped up on a pillow.

"Maybe you're right, dear, but call me the instant he starts to wake up, okay? I need to be here. He needs to know I'm here for him."

The nurse nodded a promise and ushered her to the door. Patty stopped to look back at Daniel one more time.

"I'll take care of him while you get your rest, Mrs. Richardson. I promise," the nurse said as she gently nudged her out of the room and toward the exit.

Daniel's little red car was still parked in the hospital emergency care lot. She stared at it for a few minutes, her eyes trailing the large bloodstain on the rear seat. Anger flared in her chest. Anger that they had argued. Anger that Daniel had left home like that. Anger that she didn't find him sooner. If he died, she would never forgive herself.

She called for a taxi, making a mental note to call Ned's Garage in the morning to tow her car that had stayed behind at the lake. As for Daniel's car, she'd leave it at the hospital for now, until he woke up and she knew for sure that he would recover.

When the taxi stopped in front of Patty and Daniel's home, she hesitated climbing out, second-guessing if she had done the right thing leaving Daniel alone at the hospital. The driver's eyes stared at her from his rearview mirror.

"Ma'am, this is your stop," he said looking confused.

"Of course," she mumbled slowly getting out.

The neighborhood was dark and quiet. She hurried up the path and disappeared inside the safety of her home, leery of the unknown dangers that lurked in the dark. In a few hours, the sun would rise, and the street would come alive again. She far preferred the morning scurry of everyone getting to work and school, she thought. But inside her home, everything was just as quiet and dark and suddenly as terrifying as things had seemed outside. She switched on every light on the way to her room, wondering if this was what it would be like if Daniel never came home again.

THE INCESSANT CHIMING of the doorbell woke Patty around noon the next day. She had taken a shower and fallen asleep on the bed forgetting to wrap her hair into curlers, her essential nightly ritual to get rid of the frizz in her ash blonde hair. Rushing to answer the door, she caught a glimpse of herself in the foyer mirror. She looked a mess and quickly smoothed her hair back as best she could.

"Who is it?" she called through the door.

"Mrs. Richardson, it's me, Angus," the voice came back.

Alarm bells for Daniel rang in her head as she looked back and noticed the time on the clock behind her.

"Mrs. Richardson, is everything okay? I heard what

happened," Angus said again.

Patty took a deep breath and opened the door, squinting as the sun pierced her eyes.

"Sorry, Angus, I didn't get home until the early hours of the morning. Come on in. I'll get some coffee started." She left the door open for him to follow her into the kitchen.

"How's Mr. Richardson?"

"Since I left him last night, probably the same. The nurse promised she'd call me when he wakes up."

"Is there anything I can do for you, Mrs. Richardson?"

She smiled at him as she opened a tin of her home-made granola cookies that had become his favorite.

"I think it's time you call me by my first name, don't you think? I don't hand these cookies to just anyone you know," she smiled warmly. "And you look like you haven't slept or eaten in days. Eat up," she pushed the tin under his nose.

He smiled back. "You know I can't resist these, thank you, Mrs.—sorry, Patty."

She popped two empty cups down in front of the coffee maker.

"So, what's your excuse for not getting any sleep?" she asked.

Angus rubbed the back of his neck before he reached for another granola cookie.

"It's this case I'm working on. It's got me stumped."

"Ah yes, the body in the barrel."

"You know about it?"

"The entire town is talking about it, Angus. I don't know what's happening, but since your predecessor landed behind bars, all sorts of things in this town are suddenly coming out of the woodwork. It's like the old crook covered them up or something."

"That is truer than you know. Except, as much as I don't like Hutch, I very much doubt he had any hand in this case."

Patty poured the coffee and placed the cups between them on the table.

"You're a really good sheriff, Angus. I'm sure you'll find the culprit responsible for such a heinous crime before you know it. Any idea who it was?"

Angus shook his head as he took a large mouthful of coffee, suddenly realizing that Patty might just be the person to solve a riddle.

"Say, Patty, you've been a Weyport resident for a while now, right?"

"Nearly all my life. Why?"

"I was just wondering, does the name Kim Kincaid mean anything to you?"

Angst ripped through Patty's body and the cup of hot coffee slipped out of her hand and splashed across the table. The blood drained from her face and long-buried emotions of hatred shot through her veins.

It had been a very long time since that woman's name had been spoken in her home.

CHAPTER TWENTY-TWO

Angus jumped up to get the roll of kitchen towels, his eyes searching the grim look on Patty's face.

"Are you okay?" he asked as he blotted up the coffee and righted the knocked over cup.

She snatched the paper towels from his hands and finished cleaning the mess in front of them.

"Fine," she said, barely recognizing her own voice.

"You sure? You look like you've seen a ghost."

"I'm fine. I'm just tired. I have to get back to the hospital. Thanks for stopping by."

She hurried him to the door as she dropped the soaked towels into the trash can. Angus turned to leave stopping in the doorway, his eyes both tender and suspicious as he turned to look at her.

"You've heard her name before haven't you, Patty?"

The look on her face told him he wasn't wrong but Patty didn't speak.

"Look, you can tell me. I'm just trying to figure things out with this case."

They stared at each other for several seconds. Patty's heart pounded out of control, warning her not to say too much.

"I don't know what you're talking about, Angus, sorry. Like I said, I'm tired and I have to get back to the hospital. Daniel needs me."

Guilt set in the instant the deceiving words left her mouth and she quickly brushed past Angus to let him out. With her back toward him, she told herself to keep it together, to not give anything away.

"I didn't mean to upset you," Angus said as he stepped onto the porch. "If you need anything, anything at all, you call me, okay?"

She nodded from behind the door that was already halfway closed, desperate for him to go. She hoped she had succeeded in hiding the emotions that raged within as she watched through the peephole to make sure he left. Once he had, she stood there with her back leaning against the door, an old heartache suddenly sat shallow in her chest. When the first tear rolled down her cheek, she brushed it away with a heavy hand.

"Pull yourself together, Patty Richardson! It's all in the past," she spoke to herself in a harsh tone. "It's no good dredging it all up now. Let sleeping dogs lie."

She smoothed her hair back and with head and heart in alignment again, Patty moved into her bedroom to change her clothes. She was just about done when the doorbell echoed through the house.

Panic rushed into her stomach once more. If Angus came back with more questions, she would simply not open the door. Relief washed over her when the peephole revealed Ned's friendly face instead. She opened the door to find him holding out her car keys.

"Thought you could do with some help getting your car back," he said before she could say anything.

"How did you...? I was just about to call you."

"Belinda Baxter called me first thing this morning. She told me what happened."

Patty took the keys from him.

"Thanks, Ned. Sometimes I forget how small this town is."

He laughed.

"Yeah, it's not easy keeping things quiet in this place. Also, if you need me to get Daniel's car, just holler. I noticed it's not parked in your drive."

"That's kind of you, thank you. It's still at the hospital."

She didn't tell him she couldn't bear getting inside the car again.

"Consider it done. I'll bring it later this afternoon. How is Daniel?"

"He was still unconscious when I left him last night.

His injury is quite severe. The doctor said he might not wake up for another few days."

"Was it a car accident? I can't seem to get the gossip straight."

"He was impaled by a branch, probably caused by the strong wind. He shouldn't have been out in the first place." Her mind trailed to the suspicious blood trail she had found inside his car. "I guess we'll know for sure what happened when he wakes up."

"Well, when he does, tell him I'm ready to take back the winning title in bridge. The guys are also eager to see him back. He seemed a bit distracted at the last game night with this whole lake project debacle between him and Bill."

Ned turned to leave then stopped, holding out a scrunched up brown paper bag.

"I nearly forgot. I found Daniel's coat on the ground by the lake. I'd recognize this old thing anywhere."

She took it from him.

"Believe it or not, this old thing is what helped us get out of there alive. I used it under the wheel to get his car unstuck."

Ned chuckled and tucked his hands inside his grease-stained overalls.

"You know, Daniel's always told us you're too smart for him. I must say, I agree. Not sure my wife would have thought to use a coat to get the car unstuck, and she's been watching me fix cars for nearly thirty years now. Daniel's a lucky man." He belted a laugh as he left, waving one hand up in the air behind him.

She could have argued his last statement but was eager for Ned to leave and as soon as he was out of sight, Patty rushed to her car. She cast a glance over each shoulder then popped the trunk open. The military green steel box she had dug out of the puddle was still there.

She snatched it up and hurried back inside her house, setting the box on the dinner table once inside. For a while, she just stood there staring at the rusty box that had sliced her foot open.

While she had sat at Daniel's bedside, pondering why he would risk his life to go to the land in such bad weather, it had occurred to her that she'd found what he was looking for. She had seen the dozens of holes all along his land, and the shovel in the backseat of his car, indicating that he had been looking for something.

Daniel Richardson had a secret, one that compelled him to risk his life to protect. That secret must be contained inside the box. And if she cast her reflections beyond that, the box was quite possibly also the reason he had refused to sell or develop his grandfather's land.

Bent on finding out what Daniel was hiding, Patty searched for the key to the padlock. After rummaging through every drawer and box in the house for nearly an hour, she didn't find the right key and eventually gave up, realizing he must have hidden it inside his stupid little car.

Like the day before, she wasn't going to let the car

stand in her way. She'd break the box open with a crowbar if that was what it took, and set off to Daniel's shed in search of his tools. But as soon as she stepped into her back garden, the phone rang. It was the hospital, calling her to come urgently.

"Why? Is Daniel awake?" she asked.

"He's not," the nurse said. "Mrs. Richardson, you should come immediately. I'm afraid Daniel's taken a turn for the worse."

CHAPTER TWENTY-THREE

Angus left Patty's more confused than ever. She had recognized Kim Kincaid's name, of that he was certain. What was she not telling him? Was it possible Vanessa Digby and Kim Kincaid were one and the same? Is that why Digby ran? Could it be that the two of them had faked her disappearance all those years ago? But there was still a dead body. How did she figure into all of this?

The harder Angus tried sorting through the barrage of questions swirling in his mind, the harder it became to see a connection. There were no answers.

Frustration crept into his spirit, and he pulled his car off to the side of the road, desperate to take a moment to quiet his thoughts and pray for wisdom.

Sensing the Spirit's peace again, he made a call to Tammy.

"I take it you heard," she said before he had a chance to speak.

"Heard what?" he asked, perplexed.

"About Daniel Richardson."

"What about him? Has something happened?"

"Apparently his condition has worsened. He slipped into a coma a little while ago. They're not sure if he's going to make it."

Shock ripped through Angus' insides and all he could think of in that moment was Patty and what she must be going through.

"No, I hadn't heard. I just left Patty a little while ago and she said his condition was unchanged," Angus said, feeling shocked.

"Poor woman," Tammy continued. "I mean the storm was bad but bad enough to fling a stick into his stomach? It's a terrible freak accident. I just cannot imagine what she must be feeling right now. But I'm guessing that's not why you called. Did you need me to do something for you?"

Angus took a moment to shift his thoughts back to the case before he answered.

"I need you to look into Digby's finances, specifically around eight to ten years ago."

"Didn't Miguel do that already?"

"He did but I need you to look again, with fresh eyes."

"What should I be looking for?"

"Insurance payouts, but not necessarily a lump sum. It

could even be small regular payments. The Presumption of Death Act would have gone into effect seven years after Kincaid's disappearance, meaning that any insurance would have been paid out. Call me if you find anything. I need to swing by the ME's office."

"10-4, Sheriff."

After they ended the call, Angus set off to see Murphy. He found her at her desk doing paperwork when he lightly knocked on her door.

"Hope I'm not disturbing you," he said when she briefly looked up without greeting.

"Is there something I can help you with, Sheriff Reid?" Murphy said stiffly while she continued working.

The space between them felt uncomfortable and Angus stepped in and closed the door behind him. He could not ignore the obvious.

"Can we talk, Murphy?"

"I can't stop you, so knock yourself out." Her tone was cold.

"I'm sorry about the other day and I'm sorry if you were expecting more."

"Oh, don't flatter yourself. This," she gestured back and forth between them, "was never going to work and you know it."

Her words struck a chord that left him speechless.

Murphy dropped her pen and sat back in her chair, her fingers clasped over her waist.

"You look surprised at my answer."

"I enjoy spending time with you, Murphy."

"Just as long as that time is kept professional, right? Message received. Honestly, I'm a grown woman, so let's move on, shall we? I'm assuming you're here about the Jane Doe case. A phone call would have sufficed."

"I wanted to clear the air, make sure we're okay."

Murphy snickered.

"You mean you wanted to clear your conscience. I'll make it easy for you then. We're okay, Sheriff Reid. There, your conscience is clear. Happy now?"

"I've offended you. I never meant to lead you on, Murphy. It's just, —"

"You're still not over your ex. I get it. Like I said, let's move on, shall we?"

Try as he might, Angus couldn't come up with anything more to say. Murphy had called him out on the truth. He wasn't over his ex-wife and he wasn't sure he ever would be. They had shared too much and lost too much to simply move on and act as if nothing had ever happened. Even though she had moved on from him a long time ago, he hadn't.

Murphy interrupted his thoughts.

"You wanted to talk about the case," she prompted.

He cleared his throat, still feeling awful for the embarrassment he had caused Murphy.

"I wanted to ask if you were able to extract any DNA from the body."

"Some but it wasn't conclusive. I sent it to a specialist lab to try out a new method I recently read about in a medical journal. They use next-generation sequencing to determine identity on corpses as old as forty-four years. It's quite the technological breakthrough."

Angus smiled at the way her eyes lit up when talking about identifying corpses.

"You find it funny," she said, her guard still up.

"Nope, I was just admiring your passion for your job. Your eyes lit up as soon as you went all Dr. Bones on me."

Murphy's defenses came down just enough for the corner of her lips to turn up into the tiniest of smiles.

"When do you think you'll get the results back?" Angus asked in an attempt to avoid another awkward situation.

"I'm not entirely sure. This type of testing is new to me. I don't often get pickled bodies on my table."

Angus scratched his chin.

"How about if I gave you a name? Could you see if there's a match to the tests you've already completed?"

Murphy's eyebrows lifted with curiosity.

"You have a name, already. That is quite impressive."

"It's a long shot. Just a theory I'm working on to rule out possible scenarios."

Murphy pulled her laptop closer then looked up, waiting for Angus to give her the name.

"Kim Kincaid," he said.

A frown pulled across Murphy's brows.

"Did you say Kim Kincaid? As in the woman who went missing about sixteen years ago?"

"You've heard of her?"

"Sure have. If I recall correctly, she was working for Bill Baxter at the time. She was a rookie real estate agent or something. I was a sophomore in high school when she just vanished into thin air. She was a real vixen, always dressed in these tight little dresses that showed far too much."

Murphy's jaw dropped open, and she looked at Angus with wide eyes.

"Wait! Are you thinking our Jane Doe might be Kim Kincaid?"

Angus shrugged his shoulders as he draped one leg across the corner of her desk.

"That's what I'm hoping you can verify for me, Doc."

He watched as Murphy's fingers danced across her laptop's keyboard, her face excited with prospect.

"Fingers and toes crossed. If CODIS doesn't have any DNA for Kim Kincaid on file, there's no way to know if she's the one lying in my freezer."

The printer whirred next to her and spat out a sheet of paper that she slid across the desk toward Angus.

Recognizing the protocol required to access the information on the national DNA database, Angus signed the document and handed it back to her. She pressed a few more keys then jumped up, her hands covering her mouth.

"It's her, isn't it?" Angus exclaimed when he saw her reaction and slid his leg off the desk, clasping his hands behind his head in disbelief.

Their Jane Doe had a name. The body in the barrel under the house was in fact Kim Kincaid.

CHAPTER TWENTY-FOUR

"I think you just solved a sixteen-year-old mystery, Angus!" Murphy said, her eyes still wide with excitement.

"This case is far from solved, Doc. The only thing I've done is link the two cases together and give our Jane Doe a name. But I'm no closer to finding out who killed her and why. And from where I'm standing, the killer has managed to get away with it for nearly two decades. It's not going to be easy tracking down new clues," he mused, rubbing his stubbled chin.

"Well, if it helps, Kim Kincaid wasn't the sort of woman one easily forgets. She had a certain panache that made heads turn. And when I say heads turned, there wasn't a man in this town who did not want to strike up a conversation with her. She had them all wrapped around her little finger and caused quite a stir among the women.

As teenagers, my friends and I all wanted to walk like her, talk like her, and dress like her. She loved the attention and knew exactly how to get it too. I am very certain half the town will remember a great deal about her if you ask around and, who knows, perhaps something they say will lead you to her killer. Interestingly, no one ever went looking for her when she disappeared. It was only once we saw her face on a milk carton that we realized she was gone. She always talked about how she was destined for greatness and was better suited to a life in New York. We all just assumed she had finally packed up and left for the city. It's quite ironic now that I think about it. Who would have thought someone as memorable as her could be just as easily forgotten?"

Murphy paused and slipped back behind her desk, her hands clasped atop it.

"You said earlier that she worked for Bill Baxter," Angus checked.

"As far as I remember, yes. Her face was plastered all over town and he took enormous pride in the fact that she'd come from up north somewhere to join his real estate company. And naturally, he took all the credit for her success."

"You've been a great help, Murphy, thank you. I couldn't have done it without you."

She shifted uncomfortably in her chair and busied herself with the papers in front of her.

"Glad I could help. I'm sure you'll catch the killer

soon. I'll focus my attention back to the blow to her head and see what else I can find that might help you."

"I appreciate that, thank you." he said, gesturing his appreciation with a slight nod as he left her office.

HALFWAY BACK TO HIS OFFICE, Tammy called his cellphone.

"Sheriff, I've gone through Digby's finances with a fine tooth comb and there's nothing suspicious about any of the transactions. I also checked with Kincaid's insurance companies. Her policies were never paid out. In fact, they're still lying dormant."

Angus made a grunting sound.

"I'm on my way in. Please find Miguel and meet me in the conference room, there has been a major shift in the case."

"10-4," Tammy said and hung up.

When Angus walked into his office Tammy and Miguel were waiting for him as requested.

"Right, listen up," he said as he stood in front of the evidence board.

"We've managed to put a name to our Jane Doe." He looked at Miguel where he sat eyes wide open. "Kim Kincaid," Angus said smiling as he waited for Miguel's reaction.

"You mean Vanessa Digby? But that's not possible."

"Which is precisely the reason I called this meeting.

Something just doesn't add up." Angus stuck the two women's pictures side by side on the board.

"This is Vanessa Digby, wife of our alleged home-owner, Rowley Digby. And this is Kim Kincaid, a missing person cold case dating back sixteen years."

Tammy commented next, stating what Angus and Miguel already knew.

"It's the same person," she said.

Angus drew a line between Kim Kincaid's photo and that of the body found in the barrel.

"Except, I've just had DNA confirmation that our Jane Doe is Kim Kincaid."

"Then who is Vanessa Digby?" Miguel asked.

"That's what we have to find out. Tammy, you said you didn't find any suspicious financial activity in Rowley's accounts. How about his wife, Vanessa's? As far as I can see, we have two motives here. One, insurance fraud. Second, stealing Kincaid's baby, which hopefully, forensics would back up. Mr. Digby's motive is money. He's an author with an image to uphold and he barely made ends meet back then. His wife on the other hand, was desperate for a child. Based on these financial records, there was no way they could afford IVF or a legal adoption. So, they conspired to kill Kincaid to get what they both wanted most. A two birds with one stone murder."

It doesn't matter how many theories we come up with, we don't have any evidence to back any of them up. There's nothing that confirms either of the Digbys own the house on Birch Lane. There's no evidence of insurance fraud, and we cannot prove they were anywhere near Weyport at the estimated time of death. Not to mention solving the mystery of Vanessa and our murder victim's striking resemblance, assuming no surgery was involved."

"Unless they were sisters," Miguel said. "It's right here in the adoption papers. The caseworker stated they had said the child was Vanessa's sister's and that she wasn't able to take care of him anymore."

"Of course, they'd say that because they killed this so-called sister. Besides that, I already ran a background check on both the Digbys. Neither of them have any siblings and as far as their records show, they were the only children to both of their parents."

Angus grew quiet as he stared at the evidence board.

"Miguel, let's get Mr. and Mrs. Digby in for questioning. Put them in separate rooms. The two of them had motive and since the body was found on a property Mr. Digby has access to, they are now our most likely suspects."

"I'm on it, Sheriff. I cannot wait to arrest those two."

"Let's not jump to any conclusions, Miguel. We need hard evidence before we go around accusing them. Keep your cool during the interview and let's go about this the right way this time around. He'll have his lawyer present, and we cannot afford to slip up."

Miguel dropped his head.

"Of course."

"Also, track down her next of kin. And I'd like to get a DNA test done on the child. If the Digbys don't consent to it, we'll have to get the judge to order one. I need you to get forensics back to Birch Lane," Angus said, turning to Tammy." Have them run fingerprints through whatever is left inside that house. I need evidence that Kim Kincaid was there. I know it's a really long shot, but I only need one fingerprint to prove she was alive inside the house before she got buried under it. Ask the neighbors if they had ever seen her there. Get your friend at the county office to run a check on Kim Kincaid and find out where she lived and if she owned a house. Her residence could be our crime scene. Also, it occurred to me that Birch Lane might have been leased out at some point. See if you can find any record of the property being rented out and follow the money. Check if anyone might have requested a credit score on Kim Kincaid. We need to know who owns that house. I have a gut instinct that she was killed and buried in her own house. I want no stone unturned. If you need me, I'll be at the hospital. Perhaps I can get Patty to open up. I feel awful asking her at a time like this, but she recognized our victim's name when I mentioned it earlier and I need to know what she's not telling me."

Tammy, who had been taking notes, acknowledged the instructions with a nod before they ended the meeting and went their separate ways.

CHAPTER TWENTY-FIVE

P atty stood quietly in the corner of Daniel's hospital room. Across from her, Daniel lay deathly still in his bed, a new set of tubes running between him and several more machines on either side of him. Apart from the sharp beeping of the heart monitor and rhythmic sucking of the ventilator machine, the room was quiet.

She stared at his face. He looked so peaceful. Even the usual deep frown lines had softened. She wanted to go closer, touch his face, and run her hands through his messy white hair. But she couldn't bring herself to do it. It had been so long since the last time she smoothed his hair out for him. The wedge between them had been too great.

Guilt ate at her. Perhaps she should have worked harder at fully forgiving him. Everyone deserved a second chance, even if it had wounded her so deeply. She thought she had moved on from the affair, but just hearing Angus mention that woman's name had brought all her past hurt back to the surface. She had buried it, hid from it, and prayed she'd eventually forget. And for a while, she had.

Until today.

Now, all she could dwell on were the painful memories of the day she found out about their affair. She had confronted Daniel and he had denied it, but deep inside she knew the truth. She'd always known. The signs were there, right under her nose, clear as day.

Now, it felt like she was meant to look the other way, that she was to bury the pain and the shame as if nothing had ever happened.

What had rooted instead was the fine line between hate and forgiveness. A line that stretched and strained against the weight of hurt and resentment, gnawing at her insides, torturing her soul with questions forever left unanswered.

She didn't want to hate him. She wanted to forgive him, to love him again. She had asked God many times but the hurt never quite went away.

Perhaps she didn't want it to. Perhaps she held onto the misery out of guilt. Perhaps she was to blame. Men don't stray if they are fulfilled, she believed, and she was never the kind of wife who could fully love or be loved. That future was stolen from her the night the deadbeat claimed her body without permission when she was in college. Her body was broken after that and her spirit was crushed. She wasn't able to open herself up to any man much less, give Daniel the son he'd always wanted. She had pretended to be fun and carefree, but bitterness clung to her soul like poison to the skin.

Caught up in the soul-searching turmoil that ran as a torrent within her, Patty's tears ran freely down her cheeks, unaware that Angus had popped his head around the door.

"I didn't see you there," she said, turning from him while discreetly ridding her face of sorrow as she walked to Daniel's bedside.

"You looked preoccupied, sorry. I didn't want to interrupt," Angus said as he went to stand at the foot of the bed.

Patty put on a joyful facade. "You wouldn't think he's the same grumpy old fool everyone's used to when you see him lying here so peacefully, would you?"

"How is he doing?"

"Oh, the doctors have a lot to say but, at the end of the day, they don't really know. He slipped into a coma this morning," Patty looked down at the wet tissue in her hand. "They say I should prepare myself. Whatever that means."

Angus came to stand next to her and placed his hand gently on her shoulder.

"I'm so sorry, Patty. What can I do?"

She busied herself with the bedding, smoothing it over Daniel's body.

"There's not much anyone can do, really. I'm just here, waiting." Her voice trailed off.

"You mustn't think like that, Patty. Miracles happen all around us every day. Daniel is a fighter, he'll pull through."

Just then, a doctor walked in and greeted them.

"Mrs. Richardson, do you have a moment?" he asked, clipboard in hand.

She nodded.

The doctor's eyes went to Angus.

"I don't mind you talking in front of our sheriff, Doctor. I trust him." Her eyes were warm when she looked at Angus who responded by giving her a sideways hug.

"What did you want to discuss?" Patty asked.

"We've run some further tests. Were you aware that your husband suffers from sickle cell disease?"

Patty shook her head.

"What exactly is sickle cell disease?" Angus asked when he noticed Patty appeared to be tongue tied.

"It's a rare genetic disease, most often inherited from a parent."

"His mother died from it. She had complications during Daniel's birth," Patty said dejectedly.

"That explains why Daniel has it," the doctor responded.

"What does that mean? Is it treatable?" Angus asked.

"The disease affects a person's red blood cells, producing unusually shaped cells that can cause problems such as serious infection and blocked blood vessels. We believe your husband had a stroke as a result of having this disease, exacerbated by his injury. It's unlikely he will survive unless he gets a complete bone marrow transplant. The problem with that is the donor has to be a precise DNA match. Since he has no living relatives or children, your husband's chances of matching a donor are less than slim. I realize this isn't the news you were hoping to get but we should consider preparing ourselves."

"We? You mean me," Patty said, sounding unamused.

The doctor nodded.

"And how exactly do you intend I *prepare*?"

"We, *you*, might want to consider donating his organs." The doctor handed her a pamphlet.

"If you agree, acting swiftly before death offers the recipient the best chance of survival."

The doctor paused and looked at Patty.

Angus studied her face. Her expression told him she wasn't at all impressed with the conversation and it seemed as if she could lose her temper at any second.

"Forgive me. I'm by no means qualified, but isn't it a bit soon to be discussing this? Surely there's a chance Mr. Richardson matches a donor and recovers from this?"

"There is always a chance, and we're doing everything we can for him, but we have to prepare for the alternative too. And when it comes to matters like these it is vital that, when the time comes, we act swiftly to salvage the primary organs such as his heart."

After a long and uncomfortable pause, Patty's voice was stern when she finally spoke.

"I won't do anything of the sort, Doctor. My husband isn't a quitter. He's never been ill more than a day in his life and I know he will fully recover from this. It's not in my hands to decide the number of beats of his heart or the breath in his lungs so if you're asking me to switch off these machines, it's not going to happen."

She handed the pamphlet back to the doctor.

"I realize this situation is very upsetting, Mrs. Richardson. All I ask is that you consider it while we wait."

"Wait for what exactly?" Patty asked, then continued without waiting for an answer. "I know how these things work, Doctor. The minute I sign that form I relinquish power to you and this hospital, and the decision will not be up to me anymore. You will be the one who decides when it is time to throw in the towel, not me, and there will not be a thing I can do to stop you. My answer stands. I am not signing over anything. I don't care how long it takes for my husband to wake up, but you will do whatever you must to save his life."

She leaned over and gave Daniel a peck on his forehead before she draped her purse over her forearm and walked out the door, Angus in tow.

CHAPTER TWENTY-SIX

When Patty finally stopped by the elevators on the third floor, she was next to a large window that looked down into the hospital courtyard. Gasping for air, her chest suddenly tight with angst, she tugged at the collar of her blouse.

"It's going to be okay, Patty," Angus said when he caught up with her.

"How could they even think I would switch his machines off? How could they?" she cried out through her tears.

Angus ushered her to a nearby seating area, her fragile hand in his.

"For what it's worth, I believe you did the right thing. Life and death are not in our hands. He's a doctor, looking at science and facts, trying to do what he thinks is the right thing. But we know better. Our God is the ultimate

Healer and He alone decides on whom He pours His grace. And if I'm honest, I believe, if we come before Him and ask, He will show Daniel grace too."

Angus' voice was calm and reassuring as he took both of Patty's hands in his and prayed. He prayed for her to stand firm, for the doctor to act with wisdom and sensitivity, and finally for Daniel. And when he was done, the anguish on Patty's face had been replaced with tranquility.

Leaning back in her chair, her eyes still closed and soaking up God's peace, she spoke in a quiet whisper.

"I meant it, you know."

"What?"

"I trust you. I never had the privilege of bearing a child. Daniel and I tried for many years, but it wasn't in God's plan for us. But the day I met you, it was as if our spirits connected and for the first time ever, I felt what it might feel like to have a son. I've never felt that way before. I've never met anyone like you. There's just something in your soul; your quiet strength speaks to my heart and I want to thank you for that. Your mother must be so proud of you."

Angus smiled, warmth flooding his heart as he recalls the first time she pushed her granola cookies in his hands.

"I'm here for you, Patty, for as long as God wills it. I want to help."

"You are helping," she said, squeezing his hand.

Knowing what he had to ask next, Angus briefly

looked away, unable to hide what had been weighing on him.

Patty let go of his hand and sat back in the chair, understanding in her eyes.

"It's about Kim Kincaid, isn't it?" Just saying her name jolted bitterness into her heart.

"We don't have to talk about her now, Patty," Angus said.

Patty's eyes turned toward the courtyard window as she began to talk.

"I knew God would make me deal with it again at some point in my life. We can only bury our pain for so long before He circles back to address it. And perhaps that day is today. Perhaps this situation with Daniel is how God is trying to bring me healing too. Ask what you need to know, Angus. No time like the present."

He paused for a moment, grateful that Patty was open to the topic. "Tell me how you know her."

Sadness and shame filled Patty's eyes.

"There's not much to tell, Angus. I don't know her. Frankly, I don't know if I want to either."

Angus kept quiet, silently urging her to divulge more. He needed to know the full story before he told Patty what he knew.

"The first time I laid eyes on her I knew she was trouble. It was back when Daniel and Bill were still friends and business partners. Bill had met her at some real estate convention. She used her beguiling ways to worm her way into Weyport and into their business. Bill thought she was the best thing since sliced bread. For the most part, she was very good at her job, using her sexuality to sell property like cakes at a cake sale."

Patty paused and took a deep breath before she continued. "Daniel and I were not in a good place at the time. He wanted more adventure, more attention. I didn't know how to give it. Our marriage had become strained, and he changed almost overnight, buying his flashy little red car and clothes that were much more suited for a younger man. He even took out a membership at the gym. My Daniel, who had never shown any interest in even taking a walk through the neighborhood was suddenly obsessed with fitness and the way he looked. At first, I didn't realize what was happening but looking back, the signs were all there. Kim Kincaid had lured him into her bed. It didn't matter that she was nearly twenty years younger than him, and he certainly didn't care that people were talking about their affair all over town. When our marriage finally reached breaking point, she up and left.

Daniel filed a missing person's report after she hadn't been seen for three weeks. He was convinced something bad had happened to her. But I never believed it for one minute. Anyone with eyes could see her motives. If you ask me, she had gotten everything she wanted out of Daniel, used him for whatever thrill she got from the affair, then moved on to her next victim. She set her sights on some other fool having a midlife crisis, probably in

New York where the real money is. I know at some point I'll have to face her, forgive her, but right now, I can't."

Her voice trailed off and she pulled a Kleenex from her sleeve, gently patting the corner of her eyes.

Compassion tugged at Angus' heart. He hated opening old wounds that clearly ran deep. "I'm sorry that happened to you."

"Why are you asking about her now after all this time, Angus?" Patty asked once she had composed herself. "Please don't tell me she's back in town. I can't bear seeing her, not now, not like this. Not with Daniel—"

"She's dead, Patty," Angus interrupted before her emotions ran away with her again.

Patty didn't answer and stared at him with a blank expression.

"The body in the barrel, we have confirmation that it's her. It appears she was murdered a long time ago, about sixteen years ago, in fact."

From her cold expression, Angus could tell something in Patty had changed. When she tucked her tissue back in her sleeve, threw her shoulders back, and smoothed her skirt out over her knees, his suspicions were confirmed.

"He had nothing to do with that, Angus. Daniel would never. He couldn't do something like that."

"No one is accusing him of anything."

"Yet here you are, cornering me at a time when I'm at my most vulnerable. My husband is back there fighting for his life while you're softening me up with your prayers and charm just to get me to say something that might implicate my husband in murdering that woman. You should be ashamed of yourself, Angus."

She got to her feet and started walking away.

"That's not what I'm doing, Patty. I care for you and my prayers are sincere. I'm just trying to piece everything together and find out who was responsible."

Patty turned to face him. "Then I suggest you turn your suspicions away from my husband and speak to Bill Baxter instead."

And with that, Patty turned and walked off, leaving Angus contemplating the direction his questioning had gone and considering a new suspect.

CHAPTER TWENTY-SEVEN

Patty fought to put one foot in front of the other as the storm in her head and heart raged wildly, threatening to spin out of control. The tight feeling in her chest was back, this time, accompanied by nausea in the pit of her stomach. In all this time, it had never occurred to her that Kim's disappearance was anything other than her moving on to her next target. Maybe deep down inside she had hoped or chosen to believe that Daniel had come to his senses and had broken off their affair. But never did she consider that Kim might have been murdered.

Bile pushed into her throat as she rounded the corner at the end of the hallway and she ducked into the public restroom, making it to a stall just in time. The idea that Daniel, her husband, the man she had been sleeping next to for nearly half a century, might actually be a cold blooded killer tortured her soul until her stomach ached.

She had chosen to remain faithful to him all this time, even when love wasn't always present between them. She defended him to Angus, and chose to be loyal, protecting his honor.

Because that was what a good wife was supposed to do.

All she felt was the ugly sting of betrayal.

When there was nothing left in her stomach, she turned to the small vanity and splashed several handfuls of cold water onto her face. She stared back at her reflection, droplets of water leaving streaks as they ran through her makeup.

What if she was wrong? What if Angus was right? What if Daniel had been hiding an unspeakable secret all this time?

Her thoughts turned to the steel box she had pulled from his grandfather's land. Daniel had risked his life to find something. Something she was now more certain than ever was that box and whatever it contained.

Wiping her face, her head spinning with questions, she marched back to his hospital room. The room was quiet and dimly lit, as if the doctors had moved him to the bottom of their care list, waiting to take what was left of him.

She hovered over Daniel. If he died here today, she would never know the truth. He'd take whatever was kept locked away in his head to the grave with him. And she'd be left with nothing but pain.

Determination pushed into her heart. This was not her story. This was not how her life with her husband was going to end. She wouldn't accept it.

She leaned in and whispered softly but forcefully next to his ear.

"Daniel Richardson, if you think you are going to get away with this you are sorely mistaken. You can't hide from me, not anymore. It's all out in the open now and you owe me for all the heartache you've caused. So, wake up! Wake up and face me like a man. What are you hiding in that box, Daniel, and why is it so valuable to you? Yes, I found it, I found what you went looking for so don't you dare die on me, you hear me? Don't you dare! I know you're in there somewhere. I know you can hear me. What's so important about that land, huh? Did you murder that woman? You have some answering to do, Daniel Richardson. I won't allow you to just leave me with all these questions. They have tortured me long enough."

Tears caught in her throat and stopped more words from leaving her mouth. She looked upon his face, studying it for signs of life, waiting for him to fight back. But her words had had no effect on him at all.

"Fine, if you want to be stubborn, I will go find out for myself then."

She spun around and made for the door, her determination now set on breaking open the box and putting an end to all the questions and years of agony he had put her through.

. . .

WHEN PATTY TURNED her car into her drive, she saw Bill Baxter's truck parked outside her home.

"What are you doing here, Bill?" she asked when she got out and walked toward him.

"I heard about Daniel. How is he?"

Her eyes squinted as she studied the lack of sincerity on Bill's face.

"What do you want, Bill? You and I both know that's not why you're here. It's about that stupid piece of property, isn't it? Have you come all this way to ask if my husband is dead yet? Well, he's not so you can go right back to the hole you crawled out of and forget about ever getting your hands on that land, even if he dies."

Anger rose within her and she pushed past Bill onto her porch.

"So, he is dying?" Bill said as he followed her.

Patty stopped outside her front door and spun around, furious.

"Are you taking me for a fool, Bill Baxter? How are you not ashamed of yourself? Is your love of money so deeply rooted within you that you've forgotten how to be human, how to be a friend? My husband was the one who gave you a chance, Bill. You came to Weyport all puffed up with ego looking for an opportunity and Daniel was the one who gave that to you. You would be nothing without him. Now you're standing here on the porch he built with his own two hands, waiting for him to die so you can try to take the only thing he has left of his grandfather's legacy. Get off my property! And don't you ever show your face here again, got it?"

Patty stuck her key in the lock and unlocked her front door, conscious of Bill still standing behind her. At the same time she pushed the door open wider to go inside, Bill's hand pushed firmly on her back between her shoulders. Patty stumbled forward, nearly planting face first on the floor.

"What do you think you're doing?" she yelled, catching her balance on the nearby entrance table.

Bill didn't answer. Instead, he slammed the door shut behind them. He stood in front of Patty, tall and threatening.

"Get out of my house, Bill!" she screamed, grabbing an umbrella from a nearby basket and pointing it in Bill's face.

He snatched it out of her hands with one quick move and tossed it to the floor behind him. Before she had a chance to react, he had his forearm across her chest, pushing her back against the wall.

She gasped as the force knocked her breath away.

"Where is it?" he growled.

"What? Let me go," Patty strained against the force of his arm.

"Don't play games with me, Patty. Where is the deed to the land?"

"You're hurting me! Stop!"

Bill's face was red, his eyes wild as he stared down at her.

"Answer me. Where is the deed to his grandfather's land? Either you give it to me willingly or I'll tie you up and turn this place upside down."

"I don't have it," she sobbed, fear causing her insides to tense against his violent intimidation.

"I can tell you're lying, Patty. Don't take me for a fool. This is your last chance. Where is the deed?"

She watched his eyes scan the house and thought of the box she had left on the kitchen table. If Bill found it, God only knew what he would do with whatever was inside.

"It's not here, the deed isn't here. It's at the bank," she guessed, praying that he'd fall for the misdirection.

Bill's angry eyes looked into hers, searching for the truth.

Seconds later the back of his hand struck her face.

"Liar!" he yelled.

CHAPTER TWENTY-EIGHT

Patty screamed, her cheek stinging from the blow.

Bill let go of his arm across her chest and shoved her toward the living room. Patty stumbled and fell to the floor.

"Stop crying and tell me where the deed is!"

Patty drew in a few short breaths, gasping through the sobs that seemed to be out of control, and prayed for the courage to stand up to him.

"I told you already, it's not here. Daniel keeps everything in a locked box at the bank."

Bill hunched down on one leg and pushed his angry face near hers.

"I've known Daniel for a very long time, Patty. I've worked with him, remember? Daniel has never trusted any bank, not with his money and certainly not with his most important documents."

He yanked her up by her jacket.

"Move!" Bill pushed her to one of the chairs at her dining table then down into one.

Grateful to be off her wobbly legs, she tried to reason with him.

"Why are you doing this?"

He didn't answer as he moved restlessly between the sideboard and an antique writing desk in the opposite corner, yanking open the cupboards and drawers, rummaging through each one.

Patty stayed seated in her chair at the dining table, her body taut with fear. Even if she could sneak by him, she knew she could never outrun him.

She watched as Bill moved into the living room, searching through the furniture in the small room. Next, he'd be moving his search into the kitchen. She had to stop him.

"I told you, it's not here," she said and jumped up.

Bill stopped and turned to her, the look in his eyes sending ripples of terror through her body that forced her back into her chair.

"Why are you still with him, Patty? After what he's done to you. Why are you still protecting him?"

"I'm not protecting him."

Bill let out a sarcastic chuckle.

"Oh, come on, Patty. That foolish husband of yours humiliated you. He pranced around town with Kim on his arm like a peacock. Like he'd won the jackpot over every other man in this town who drooled over that woman as if she was the last female on the planet."

"So this is about you being jealous then, is it?"

Suddenly Bill was in front of her again."Jealous! Of what? This is about dignity, doing what's right. That man doesn't have a compassionate bone in his body," Bill continued angrily. "His only concern has ever been for himself and his so-called family legacy. That's all he's ever cared about. Are you honestly going to sit here and let him get away with how he treated you? The way I see it, you have the perfect opportunity to set things right, to take back what he's taken from you. All you have to do is persuade him to sell me the land."

Bill attempted to rile her up and turn against her husband. His wild eyes flecked with greed scared her and if she didn't know better, she thought she also spotted a thread of desperation.

Tears started to well up in Patty's eyes, bringing with it eighteen years of shame. Bill was right. Why would she still protect Daniel? Why defend his honor after what he'd done to her, after the shame he'd brought over her.

When she looked up at Bill something in his eyes had changed and suddenly he was in the chair beside her.

"I can't," she simply answered, her voice low as she watched her fingers twist the white fringe of her tablecloth.

"Yes, you can, Patty! He's going to have the last laugh at your expense again. Why would you let him?"

His face was up close, his voice confident as if he was masterfully putting together a property deal. She wanted to push Bill away, out of her face, and shout for him to leave her alone.

"Daniel is dying. He's in a coma. I can't make him do anything," she heard herself say out loud for the first time.

She watched Bill frown as he sat in the chair next to her, an unfamiliar emotion evident in his eyes. Patty searched more closely. It was fear. Bill Baxter was scared. But why?

"What have you done, Bill?" she asked, comprehension beginning to dawn.

Bill shot up and paced the small space around the dining table, his hands in his hair.

"What did you do?" Patty pushed.

"I never, it wasn't..." he stuttered without making any sense.

"Never what?"

Stopping on the other side of the table, Bill peered out into the street in front of the house.

"It was an accident, Patty. You have to believe me. I never meant for him to get hurt. He's just so stubborn. If only he didn't come at me..."

She frowned with confusion.

"What are you saying, Bill?"

He started pacing the small space then looked full into her face. The wild expression on his face told Patty that a storm was raging inside him. And the look filled Patty with trepidation.

"I don't know what exactly you're saying, but we can talk it through."

"I told you; it was an accident. He came at me first and the stick—"

He stopped mid-sentence, as if he suddenly realized what he was confessing, then dashed to the desk and yanked open one of the small drawers.

When she saw his hands holding the ball of red and white twine she used to wrap gifts her heart skipped several beats.

"What are you doing? No! Stop!" she yelled out when he pulled her arms behind the chair. His strong hands gripped her wrists, and he started wrapping the twine tightly around the wooden slats and her wrists .

"Bill don't do this, please!"

But he ignored her and instead reached for a cloth napkin from the sideboard and gagged her mouth.

She moaned from under the crisp white Damask fabric and watched him move down the hallway and into the master bedroom.

She unsuccessfully wrestled against the strain of the cord around her wrists.The corners of her mouth hurt, and she tried to push the fabric out with her tongue. She wanted to scream for help and shout at him to leave. Instead, the only sounds that escaped from behind the fabric were pitiful moans.

Her body fell into a heap in the chair, her head forward onto her chest as her moans turned into quiet sobbing.

So, she did the only other thing she could do to make it all go away. She prayed.

CHAPTER TWENTY-NINE

Angus steered his car into the parking lot in front of Bill's office. Patty's accusations still hadn't left his mind and it troubled his conscience. The last thing he had intended was to insult or hurt her. He should have never let her walk away without clearing the air between them.

He pushed aside his guilt and leaned over his steering wheel to look at the giant billboard that took up one corner of the lot. It displayed Bill standing arms crossed sporting a wide grin, a mockup of the lake development in the backdrop. He'd always been careful not to judge people, but Bill was one person who tested his resolve. The man oozed deceit and it made his skin crawl. He'd much rather pull out a fingernail than listen to Bill's clever lies.

He silenced his mind, shut his eyes, and asked for wisdom and guidance.

When a minute later Angus still couldn't bring

himself to get out of his car to walk into Bill's office, he forced himself to question why. It was as if his spirit was telling him not to.

This case had been keeping him awake at night and the pressure to solve it was coming at him from all angles. If everything went his way during the questioning, he'd have at least one of the Digbys in custody before the sun set. Everything was pointing to them being the most likely to have killed Kim Kincaid. They both had strong motives; they might even have had the means. Except, he had no evidence to support any of his suspicions and none of it mattered unless he could prove beyond doubt that they had done it.

He glanced up at Bill's face again. Patty had hinted that Bill knew something about Kim's disappearance and he couldn't ignore this new piece of information even if he wanted to.

If nothing else, he owed it to Kim to pursue all leads until one led to her killer. She deserved a proper burial. And, as an officer of the law, he owed it to her family to give them the peace they deserved.

Something he and his mother never had.

And if solving the case meant he'd have to face the likes of Bill Baxter, then so be it. He couldn't allow the man's personal flaws to interfere with his duty.

Resolving to walk into Bill's office to get to the truth, he got out of his vehicle and started walking toward the entrance. As he looked around at the cars that were parked in front of the building, his eyes fell on a vacant space that had Bill's name on a plaque in front of it. It was obvious Bill wasn't in. Angus smiled as peace washed over him.

He turned around, walked the few steps back to his car, and slid behind the wheel. Moments later his cellphone rang, and he glanced at the number on the screen.

"Hope I'm not interrupting, Sheriff, but you said you wanted to know if we found anything new," Tammy announced with excitement. "The forensics team lifted several prints in the Birch Lane house. Most were immediately ruled to be from the work crew, but there were a couple of really old partial prints in the kitchen. They're running them through the database as we speak although they did warn that they might not have enough data points. We're going to need a small miracle here, but hopefully we get a hit on them. Also, Miguel said the Digbys and their lawyer will be here in a few hours."

"Thanks, Tammy, good work. Any feedback on the ownership of the house?"

"Absolutely nothing. There's zero trace of anyone owning that property. Even the land under it shows no ownership records whatsoever. Honestly, I don't know how something like this can slip through the cracks. I have the entire clerk's desk at the county office scrambling for answers."

"Well, keep on it, please, and have them rush those prints. I might only have one shot at getting the Digbys to confess. I'll make my way in shortly."

"10-4."

After they had ended the call, Angus dialed the number for the hospital. His spirit nagged at him to set things right with Patty and he couldn't let it go.

When he asked to be put through to Daniel's room, the nurse told him Patty had already left and gone home.

Angus glanced at the clock on his dashboard. He decided he had time. The Digbys wouldn't be arriving for another few hours. Patty needed a friend and he needed to clear his conscience. He drove toward Patty's house, praying God would give him the right words to say when he got there. At the very least, he owed her an apology.

As he drove past the local flower shop, the fresh flowers in the window caught his eye and he decided that Patty could do with a bit of cheer. The florist behind the counter was as friendly as the fresh peonies she was busy arranging.

"Hello, Sheriff. Looking for something special?" asked the woman he guessed to be in her late forties.

"I sure am. Do you have something suitable for an apology?"

"Do I?" she mocked. "Nothing says 'I'm Sorry' quite like a beautiful bunch of white tulips. It signifies the desire to start new. Shall I tie up a bunch for you?"

Angus nodded.

"That will be great, thank you."

"Would you like a card to go with that?"

"No thanks, I prefer delivering apologies in person."

Angus watched as she skillfully started pruning a bunch of tulips.

"Would you mind if I pick your brain a bit, please... Lily-Mae," he asked as he read her name badge, thinking there could not be a more appropriate name for a florist.

"Sure thing. Fire away," her bubbly answer returned.

"Have you been living in Weyport long?"

"Me? I was practically born here. Why?"

He angled his body to make sure he got a full view of her face that had been slightly obscured behind the flowers before he continued.

"Does the name Kim Kincaid mean anything to you?"

Lily-Mae stopped cutting midway through a stem, her face filled with surprise.

"Wow, now that's a name I haven't heard around here for a while."

"So, you know of her then."

"You would've had to have been under a rock if you didn't. I have her to thank for one of my most successful Valentine's Days ever." She laughed. "I'm sure she's got the entire city of New York sending her bunches of flowers every day. I hope she comes back. She was good for business."

Her answer surprised Angus.

"You think she's in New York."

"Of course. She never stopped talking about living her best life in the Big Apple." Lily-Mae lowered her scissors noisily on the wooden bench between them as she looked up at Angus, her eyes suddenly wide with curiosity.

"Wait, why are you asking about her? I heard you found a body in her house. Was it hers?"

Excitement ripped through Angus and he could hardly get the next question out.

"Her house - she owned a house on Birch Lane?"

"Yes. Isn't that where you found the body? The entire town's talking about it just like they did back when Bill and Daniel gave it to her. It had a lot of tongues wagging back then."

CHAPTER THIRTY

A ngus stood in stunned disbelief as he tried to digest what Lily-Mae was telling him.

"You look shocked. Did you not know?"

"No. What do you mean they gave her the house? Why would they do that?"

She threw her head back as she laughed.

"If you had met Kim Kincaid, you wouldn't have asked me that question. She had the men in this town eating out of the palm of her hand. They were like a litter of puppies running after her, each trying to impress her with bigger and better gifts. Oh, and the number of flowers I delivered to that house. I had to rent a truck just to get all the flowers to her on Valentine's Day. I had cramps in my hand for a week from writing out all the cards."

She pulled the small bunch of tulips together with a

neat bow as Angus stood there taking in what she was telling him.

"What about Bill Baxter? Did he send her any flowers?"

"And risk being clobbered over the head with a pan by Belinda? He's too much of a wimp for that. Bill only sends flowers to his clients. The cheap ones," she said, winking.

He handed her cash to pay for the tulips and she placed the bouquet of tulips on the counter in front of him.

"And you're sure she lived at 16 Birch Lane."

"I'm positive. Better yet, I'll show you."

Lily-Mae disappeared behind a tall bookshelf to what he assumed was her office. She popped back out from behind the bookcase a few minutes later and dropped a thick binder that was covered in layers of dust on the counter.

"This is the binder with the receipts for all my deliveries made during the time she was here. Sorry for the dust, it's been a while since I've had to open this one." She smiled then flipped through half a dozen page flags before she landed on the one she was looking for.

"See here," she pointed to the address written in faded ink at the top of the receipt. "Deliver to Miss Kim Kincaid, 16 Birch Lane." She turned the page. "So was this one, and this one, and all of these," she said as she ran her thumb through a wad of receipts.

Angus angled his head to read the text next to her

finger, eventually turning the binder all the way around. There were hundreds of receipts, all ordering flowers to be delivered to Kim at the Birch house.

"I can't believe you kept these."

"You bet. Every single delivery I've ever made since I opened Blooms twenty-five years ago. I keep track of everything. Blame my OCD," she giggled.

"This is extremely helpful. I might need to hold onto these receipts if that's okay. I'll get them back to you of course."

"With pleasure." She pulled them out of the binder and slipped them into a brown paper bag. "If you need anything else you know where to find me." She gave a sweet smile.

"I appreciate that. Thanks for your help, Lily-Mae, and for these," Angus said holding up the bouquet.

"Anytime, Sheriff. I hope they do the trick." She leaned in and whispered, pointing her eyes at the paper bag with receipts in his hand. "By the way, most of those were placed by the same man. I remember Kim always smiled the biggest when she got flowers from Daniel Richardson. She had a soft spot for him like no other. We all thought he was going to leave Patty for her but then Kim moved to New York so luckily that never happened."

Angus stared at the bag of receipts before he looked at Lily-Mae, a questioning frown on his forehead.

"Wait, what are you saying? You knew about Daniel Richardson and Kim's affair?"

She nodded, her nose all scrunched up then said, "It was quite the scandal back then, considering she was nearly half his age. Everyone knew, most of us long before Patty even had an inkling. And Daniel didn't even try to hide it. The disrespect! Poor Patty, I don't know how she lived down the humiliation that must have caused her. But she did and thankfully, it all died down after Kim left town. I'm glad they could move on from it. Pity things have taken a turn for the worst with him, though. Who would have thought a freak accident would be the reason their marriage ended."

Just then another customer walked in and Lily-Mae stopped talking, putting an end to the gossiping tone her conversation had taken on. Before long she thanked Angus for his business and moved on to the mother and daughter duo who stood in wait behind him.

Back in his car, Angus tried to digest all the information he had just gathered. He stared at the bunch of tulips he'd dropped in the seat next to him. His heart ached for what Patty had gone through back then and regret for opening old wounds at a time she least needed it, tugged at the back of his mind.

He rubbed at his forehead as another nasty thought nagged at him. If Patty knew about the affair and watched as Daniel flaunted it all over town, she'd have the perfect motive to kill Kim too.

His shoulders and neck ached with tension as he wrestled with the prospect of having to treat Patty as another suspect to Kim's murder. No amount of tulips would ever be enough to mend the rift if he so much as started to question her about it. He dropped his head back against the headrest. He'd wait and see how things played out with the Digbys. For now, he would help her get through the trauma with Daniel.

And pray to God that he was wrong about suspecting her.

He turned his car back onto the road and headed toward Patty's house. The short drive delivered him there quickly and as he entered her neighborhood, summoned the courage he needed to face her. Approaching her house, he saw Bill's branded luxury pickup truck parked out front. When he pulled up behind it, he noticed that Bill wasn't in the truck. He scanned Patty's house next, noticing a plant on the porch next to her front door had been knocked over. Brushing it off as one of the casualties from the storm, he turned off his car and scooped up the tulips. If, considering Daniel's condition, Patty and Bill had decided to call a truce between them after all these years, he might have the opportunity to question both of them after all. An informal approach appeared to be the best tactic under the circumstances, Angus thought in preparation.

He rang the doorbell and waited. When Patty didn't answer the door, he rang it again, followed by a quick knock. From behind the door, there was a thump, then silence. He waited. No response.

"Hello, Patty, it's me, Angus," he yelled out, as worry started building in his mind.

Still, no one answered.

He moved over to the window and peered through the lace drapes then tapped lightly on the window.

"Patty, I just wanted to say I'm sorry for what happened this morning," he started, then spotted a shadow moving in the living room.

Unease nagged at his insides, and he moved back to the door where he knocked a bit harder this time.

At the sound of glass breaking, his body went into full alert, knowing something was out of place.

Laying the tulips against the overturned planter, he reached for the doorknob.

CHAPTER THIRTY-ONE

Angus moved slowly, cautious of what danger might lurk on the other side of the door. Surprised that the door was unlocked, he gently opened it. The wood of the door was swollen from the rain and scraped over the worn doorpost as he inched it open with his fingertips. He paused, listening for movement. When he heard no other sounds, he pushed the door farther until it was fully open. With one hand still on the door, he placed his other hand atop his holster, ready for whatever might surprise him.

From inside the house, the floor creaked. He stopped and listened. Silence.

"Patty," he called out in a loud whisper.

Muffled moaning came at him from somewhere close by.

Angus moved quickly through the house. He stopped at the corner of the hall just before he would need to turn left to enter the dining room. He had detected that was the direction from where he had heard the moaning.

He heard movement, Patty's muffled sounds, and then heavy panting. Angus slowly pulled his gun from his holster.

Was Bill with her? Was he holding her under duress? Had he hurt her?

Angus closed his fingers tighter over his gun and pressed his back against the wall. His heart thudded in his ears, his body tense and ready to react.

More whimpering.

More heavy breathing.

He needed to act.

"I just want to talk, Bill."

"Go away, Sheriff!" Bill yelled back.

It was the confirmation Angus needed. Bill was there and Patty was in trouble.

"Bill, don't do anything foolish. Whatever you're trying to do here we can talk about it."

"My business isn't with you. Just turn around and leave. I'm not going to hurt her. I just want—"

Bill stopped mid-sentence.

Angus heard shuffling, as if Bill was dragging Patty along with him.

"You just want what, Bill? Let Patty go and I'll help you get whatever you're here for."

Bill didn't respond.

"Okay, I'm coming out to talk, face to face. No one wants anything bad to happen here today."

"No! Go away! I'll leave when I'm done finding what I came here for. I don't want to hurt her, Sheriff, but I will if I need to."

"And then what? Where are you going to hide? You and I both know I'll have to arrest you. Be it tomorrow or the next day I'll find you so why not just end this now?"

Bill fell silent and Angus hoped Bill was considering what he had just said.

Angus gave him a few more seconds then announced that he was coming out."If you are armed, Bill, drop your weapon. I'm putting my gun away. Let's talk about this."

Angus holstered his gun, leaving the clip undone just in case. When he was ready, he held out both his hands where Bill could see them.

"See, I'm unarmed, Bill, I'm coming out."

Angus took a deep breath and slowly came out from behind the wall. When he rounded the corner, he saw them. They were backed into the corner on the other side of the dining table, the semi open kitchen to their left.

Bill had his forearm wrapped around Patty's chest, pulling her into his body to use as a shield. Her mouth was gagged, and her hands tied behind her back. In Bill's other hand, he was holding tightly to a military green steel box, clutching it like a football under his arm. Patty's eyes met Angus', fear in her gaze that clearly pleaded for help.

Angus had both his hands out in front of him as if he

was searching for something in the dark. He moved slowly, closer to the table.

"Stop!" Bill yelled. "Don't come any closer or I'll hurt her!"

Angus stopped, glancing at Bill's hands to see if he had a weapon. On the table in front of them lay an antique letter opener, the sharp point glistening in the pale light from the nearby window.

"Okay just stay calm. Like I said, I don't want any trouble. Just let Patty go."

Bill's body was tense, his arm gripping Patty tighter into his chest. His eyes went to the gun on Angus' hip then darted back at Angus.

"I'm not planning on using it, but it's entirely up to you. Let Patty go and we don't have to find out."

Bill snickered.

"I wasn't born yesterday. I know a tactic when I see one. Besides, I already told you, I'm not leaving here until I have what I came for."

Angus dropped his gaze to the metal box under Bill's arm.

"I'm guessing you found it already, so let Patty go."

Bill's arm curled tighter around the box.

Patty moaned from under the gag.

"You're hurting her, Bill. Why drag Patty into this? Let her go."

Bill's eyes frantically scanned the rest of the house.

He leaned to the left, placing the box on the counter

separating the kitchen and the dining room, knocking his head on the overhanging cupboards that divided the two rooms. He swore under his breath and quickly snatched up the letter opener.

Angus' hand went to his gun, pausing it over his holster.

"Put it down. We had an agreement."

"No, that was all your idea, Sheriff. I never agreed to anything. This isn't a negotiation either. I told you; I would hurt her if I had to. I'll fight for what's owed to me. I've worked too long and hard to lose everything because of Daniel and his stubbornness."

He switched the letter opener into the hand that lay across Patty's neck and held the pointed end close to her throat. She moaned, her eyes wide, heightened with fear.

Bill reached back and scooped the box up under his arm once more.

"Now get out of my way or Patty will pay the price," he warned.

Bill's crazed eyes told Angus he would follow through on his threat and, with the letter opener dangerously pointed against Patty's neck, he couldn't risk making a move.

"Fine, just take it easy, Bill," he said as he slowly backed into the foyer.

Bill angled out of the corner behind the eight-seater dining table, pulling Patty closer into his chest with the letter opener still firmly pushing up against her neck.

"Get away from the door, move!" he yelled at Angus.

Angus did what he demanded and backed up into the living room instead.

When Bill had shuffled them into the open hallway, Angus knew he had to do something to stop him from getting away.

"What's in the box? What's so important that you'll risk everything, your entire life for the contents of that box?"

Bill's eyes narrowed.

"Whatever it is, Bill, I am very certain it's not worth dying over."

"Maybe to you but not to me. This is the only thing standing between me and my dreams and I am not prepared to give it up. I have a lot riding on the Lakeview project, and I won't let Daniel take that from me too. Besides, as I understand it the old fool is dying so he won't need the land anyway."

Angus needed to switch gears and fast.

"Where is Kim Kincaid, Bill?"

Bill gasped as the unexpected question knocked the breath from him.

"You're not pinning that on me. I had nothing to do with her death, you hear me? Nothing!"

Angus cocked his head to one side, his eyes narrowed with suspicion.

"Who said she was dead, Bill?"

CHAPTER THIRTY-TWO

A flustered look settled on Bill's face as if he'd just been caught stealing a cookie from the cookie jar.

"Everyone knows she's dead."

"Not quite. Most of the people in this town are saying she's alive and well and living her best life in New York. How do you know she's dead?"

Angus paused, waiting for Bill to say more. To slip up again. Except he didn't.

So, Angus pushed harder.

"Because you did it. You killed her."

"Kill her? Are you insane?" Bill exploded, beads of sweat stippling his forehead.

"You were jealous of her affair with Daniel. So, you killed her, out of jealousy," Angus prodded.

"Jealous, that's ridiculous! I have never been jealous of Daniel. I was the one who discovered her, not him! He never had the business acumen to recognize a good opportunity when it came his way. I did. She was worth gold to our business. *I* found her and offered her a job in our business. She worked for me and was an asset to my team. Nothing more. And she was really good for business. Why would I kill her? Daniel was like half the other men in this town, mesmerized by her beauty. It was embarrassing to watch. He was old enough to be her father and the way he behaved was a disgrace to our business, but I never killed her."

Patty whimpered from under Bill's grip and Angus tried to console her with his eyes when Bill wasn't looking.

"Is that why the two of you had a falling out? You wanted what Daniel had? You said it yourself; you found her. She was yours, not his."

Bill lost his temper, his body suddenly wild with rage.

"No! I told you already, I wasn't jealous."

"Then why did you split up? Why the animosity between you and Daniel?"

"Because he accused me of killing her just like you are now!" Bill shouted. "He just couldn't accept the fact that she left him and was never going to come back, so he blamed me for everything. But I told him just like I'm telling you now; I had nothing to do with her death. Nothing, you hear me!"

Emotion had gotten the better of Bill and in his outburst the box slipped out from under his grip. He reacted, unthinking, and reached to catch it, involuntarily loosening his grip on Patty.

Angus charged toward them, shoved Patty out of the way, and jumped on top of Bill, pushing him onto the floor.

Bill groaned as he fell on top of the steel box.

Angus wrestled to keep him down, but Bill gained leverage and rolled himself off the box.

Bill threw a punch, landing it squarely on Angus' jaw. Angus lost his grip on Bill who seized the moment and plowed into Angus. The two fell back onto the floor.

Angus reached for his gun while wrestling against Bill's weight. Bill caught the movement and reached for the weapon as well. They vied for the gun, pushing against each other's physical strength.

Angus fought back, stared into Bill's wild eyes.

A single gunshot echoed through the house.

The struggle ceased, and neither man moved.

Muffled shrieks from Patty drifted toward them.

Bill moved.

Angus lay still on the floor.

Patty watched in horror, her eyes wide with shock when Bill looked up at her.

"I didn't...I'm sorry, Patty, this wasn't supposed to happen." Bill's voice was heavy, partly regretful, mostly full of fear.

He scrambled to his feet and snatched up the box that lay on the floor a few feet away. When he got his bearings, he looked at Patty where she had wedged herself into the corner, her mouth still gagged, her hands still tied behind her back.

"I didn't want this, any of this. You should have just given me the deed to the land then none of this would have happened," Bill said, turning to look back at Angus who was still laying on the floor.

Patty moaned from under the gag, her eyes pleading for him to let her go.

Bill paced the small area around Angus, stepping over the blood that was seeping out from his shoulder and pooling under his body.

Reality set in and Bill started to panic.

He looked at the gun on the floor, then at Patty. Grasping his plan, she shook her head, her eyes begging him to let her go.

"You know I can't let you live, Patty. You were the only one who saw what happened here. I won't go to prison for any of this."

He picked up the gun and aimed it directly at Patty.

She moaned, shook her head, and sobbed uncontrollably into the gag.

"I'm sorry. You left me with no other choice."

Bill's shaking hand lifted and took aim. His finger squeezed down on the trigger.

Patty let out a muffled scream.

Something smashed into Bill's knee from behind,

causing his legs to give way under his body. The bullet went flying into the wall next to Patty's head.

Bill groaned and looked back as he fell to the floor. Angus had kicked his leg out from under him, stopping him from killing Patty.

Bill cussed, then turned from his position on the floor, and pointed the gun at Angus to take another shot at him, to finish him off.

But Angus was ready and kicked Bill's face, sending him back across the floor instead. The gun slid underneath the nearby sofa, out of reach for both of them.

Angus winced as the pain from the bullet wound in his shoulder caught up with him and he closed his hand over it. Blood seeped from his arm and settled in the spaces between his fingers. Bill seized that opportunity and moved to tackle him, aiming to strike Angus over the head with the steel box.

Angus ducked, pushing Bill off kilter which caused him to lose his grip on the box.

"Run, Patty!" Angus screamed at her as Bill scrambled after the box, clearing her path to the front door.

But Patty didn't move.

"Patty run, get out!" Angus shouted again as he latched onto Bill's body to hold him down.

From the corner of his eye Angus saw her rush toward them. Moments later she planted her foot into Bill's side.

He groaned and swore at her, trying to pull her to the floor. He missed. She kicked him again, this time harder.

Angus clambered on top of Bill, shoving his knee between Bill's shoulder blades, and pushed his face down into the floor.

Patty circled them and kicked the steel box out from under Bill's fingertips where he had been clinging onto it. The motion made her lose her balance and she fell back onto the couch, bumping her head on one of the corners.

Angus strained to keep Bill down under his knee and good arm, but he was losing blood and strength.

Bill searched for a way out, his eyes darting between the box and the front door.

In one quick movement, Bill pushed Angus off his back and scrambled to his feet, this time choosing freedom over the box.

Seconds later he ran out of the door and escaped, his truck's wheels screeching in the road as he raced off.

CHAPTER THIRTY-THREE

Angus pushed himself off the floor, the wound in his shoulder shooting agonizing stabs of pain through his body. Patty lay halfway across the sofa, her body shaking from the horror she'd just suffered.

"It's okay, Patty. It's going to be okay," Angus consoled her as he pulled the fabric restraint from her mouth and freed her hands before calling in the incident.

She sank forward onto his chest and sobbed. She sobbed for what had just happened, for what she had gone through with Daniel's injury, and for all the shame and misery she'd had to endure for years.

"Help is coming," Angus said, groaning with pain.

"I'm so sorry, Angus," she said, her eyes filled with shame and guilt. She pressed the fabric gag to his shoulder to try to stop the blood.

"It wasn't your fault."

"Yes, it was. I should have told you about the box when I told you about Kim."

Angus leaned back against the foot of the sofa.

"Nothing you could have told me would have stopped Bill from coming here, Patty. He was after whatever is inside that box." He groaned then added, "So, are you going to tell me, or must I get shot a second time?"

Patty smiled then glanced at the box that lay a few feet away.

"Truth be told, I don't have any idea what's inside that stupid box. I found it buried in the sand out on Daniel's land by the lake. That's what I cut my foot on when I was trying to get my car unstuck. I figured it was what Daniel had been looking for when I saw all the holes around his property. So, I brought it home. For some strange reason Bill thought it was where Daniel kept the deed to the piece of land."

"So that's why Bill came here. To get the deed to the land."

Patty nodded as fresh tears trickled down her pale cheeks.

"I've never seen Bill act this crazy. If you hadn't come, he would have killed me," Patty said as a fresh wave of sorrow hit her.

"It was all God's doing, Patty. I hadn't planned to come here but I felt so bad for what I'd said to you at the hospital. I came here to apologize to you. It was insensitive of me and I'm sorry."

Patty stroked his face and gave him a tender smile.

"You're just doing your job. Daniel might be many things but a killer he is not. He could never. He loved her far too much for that."

Patty looked down at her lap, her face showing years of pain.

"I'm sorry Daniel did this to you, Patty. My father wasn't faithful to my mother either. Though most of the time his love of liquor had more to do with it than the women. Yet, you chose to forgive Daniel, to stay with him. That shows strength. My mother opted not to. Instead, she fled, from the shame, the country she loved, everything."

"Sounds like you had a tough childhood and some forgiveness of your own to work through."

She stared at her wedding photo displayed on the nearby cupboard before she continued.

"I don't think I ever did forgive him, Angus. Just like death, one learns to live with the things that hurt us most. The regrets, the sadness, the empty numb feeling it leaves behind. That's all I've done all these years. Survived. Pretended nothing ever happened. It's not as if I didn't try to forgive him. God knows I've tried many times to move past the hurt and the anger. But every time he looked at me, as if he wished he was with her instead, it was a fresh reminder that I wasn't who he wanted, loved and wished he could spend the rest of his life with. I knew a long time ago that Daniel could never love me the same way he loved her. She'd put a spell on him, one that will never let him go for as long as he lives."

"Well, he doesn't know what he's been missing out on. You are one of a kind, Patty Richardson."

She smiled tenderly.

"It's a pity he won't be around to find out. Daniel will never have the opportunity to love me or anyone else again. What a sad twist of fate. The legacy he's worked his entire life to preserve turned on him, claiming his life instead. Bill was right about one thing. Daniel is as stubborn as they come and if only he wasn't blinded by Kim's wiles, who knows what could have been."

"We will keep praying for him, for a miracle."

Patty lifted the blood-drenched fabric from his wound.

"We need to get you to the hospital, Angus. You've lost a lot of blood."

"It's worse than it looks, I'll live. Besides, I need to get back to chasing down Kim's killer. From what I understand she cast a spell on a lot of people in this town and that just blew my investigation wide open. Who in this town was jealous enough to want to kill her? And if jealousy was the motive, why not kill Daniel instead? That would make a whole lot more sense to me than a possessive admirer."

He left his questions hanging, not daring to ask Patty if she could have killed Kim. She'd been through enough.

The sound of approaching sirens told him help was

close by. As they waited, Patty's tender eyes locked onto his.

"The real question you should be asking yourself is what you intend to do about the high walls you've built around your heart. I've seen the way Murphy looks at you. You like her too, yet you keep her at a distance. Why? If you learn any lessons from my circumstances, learn this one: life is too short not to let love into your heart. However crooked that love might be. You owe it to yourself to put the past behind you and embrace love when it comes your way. True love doesn't come around often."

Patty sat there cradling his head on her lap, her hand pressed down on his open wound as her words of wisdom washed over him. He thought about the unseen wounds that lay hidden in his heart. Wounds that had not yet healed. Wounds he was not sure would ever fully heal until he knew the truth about his brother.

But what he did know was that this case brought about the prospect of a new angle to finding his brother—dead or alive. One that might have been right in front of him all along.

CHAPTER THIRTY-FOUR

When Angus woke up the next morning, he was still in the hospital. As his mind slowly caught up with his surroundings, he saw that he was alone in the room. Across his shoulder, a large dressing covered most of his arm and he reached over to adjust the sling that held his arm in position.

"You were lucky, Sheriff," a male voice came from the doorway. "That bullet just missed your subclavian artery. Not only that, but it also only went through muscle and there was a clean exit wound. I'd say that in itself was a miracle."

Angus smiled at the doctor who now stood at the foot of his bed checking his chart.

"How are you feeling?" the doctor asked.

"Like I've been sleeping for an entire week."

"That's the beauty of sedation. You should take it easy,

and I would suggest you make sure you carry through with the physical therapy."

"Does that mean I can go? I'm kind of in the middle of a case."

The doctor glanced at the IV bag next to his bed.

"We've got you on IV antibiotics, but I see no reason to keep you here once that bag is empty. Your vitals are stable, and I can prescribe something for the pain, as long as you promise to stick to doing deskwork for now. And I want to see you back here in a week. Agreed?"

"Agreed, thank you."

As the doctor left, Miguel popped his head around the door.

"You had us running scared there for a bit, Sheriff," Miguel said as he walked over to the bed.

"I would never miss out on catching a killer and closing a cold case," Angus joked before he turned serious. "Bring me up to speed, please."

"I've got an APB out on Bill Baxter and we're watching his house. He's hiding out somewhere but I'm confident we'll find him soon."

"That's good to hear. What about the Digbys?"

Miguel took a seat next to Angus.

"I took the liberty of proceeding with Mr. and Mrs. Digby's interviews. That lawyer of theirs is quite a character. Turns out he's nothing more than a graduate fresh out of law school. He's an intern at one of the big name firms in Boston but throws his weight around as if he's been defending serial killers all his life. He's a bag of hot air, in my opinion. Nonetheless, I managed to separate the couple and got one significant piece of information that's going to rock your world. Are you ready for it?"

Angus shot him an annoyed look.

"Fine, fine, since time isn't on our side, I'll just tell you. As it turns out, Vanessa Digby is not Kim Kincaid like we thought."

"You mean she's not an imposter who had facial reconstruction done?" Angus mocked.

"Even better! She's her identical twin!"

Angus frowned.

"Twins?"

"Yeah, Vanessa told me herself and Rowley confirmed it."

"But Tammy ran checks on her and confirmed she was an only child. Why would there not be a record of it anywhere?"

"According to Vanessa, her biological mother had given them both up via private adoption. She and Kim were separated at birth. She went in search of her biological parents with one of those ancestral DNA tests. She discovered that her mother had already passed away from a drug overdose and that she had an identical twin sister. She never found her biological father but she did reach out to her sister."

"Kim."

"Correct. The two met up about seventeen years ago

and bonded instantly. Shortly after, Kim arrived at their door one morning announcing she was pregant and that she needed a place to stay until the baby was born. Considering the Digbys' inability to have children of their own, they didn't hesitate to take her in. But as soon as the baby was born, Kim would disappear for weeks on end, leaving the baby with the Digbys. Vanessa wanted Kim to move to Nashville permanently but Kim had told her she'd met the man of her dreams right here in Weyport and that they were going to get married. Then one day Kim never returned and vanished into thin air. Neither of the Digbys ever saw or spoke to her again. Since Kim hadn't put down the father's name on the child's birth certificate, they adopted him a year later. Rowley Digby came back here to Weyport several times over the years looking for Kim at the only address they had for her. They ended up just claiming her house as theirs. Naturally, being the crime writer he is, Rowley made it his mission to keep searching for Kim. But, of course, he never found her until the contractors discovered the body under the house. Both swear they had no idea she was dead or who Kim's mystery man was."

"Thanks to my conversation with Patty, that is no longer a mystery. It was Daniel Richardson."

Miguel's mouth dropped open.

"Yeah, believe it. The two had had an eighteen-month long affair. The entire town knew it too."

"Poor Mrs. Richardson. Obviously, she didn't know until yesterday's debacle with Bill."

"Actually, she did. I can't imagine the humiliation that must have caused her." Angus' voice trailed off.

"She did a great job at hiding it." Miguel paused, his eyebrows lifted as he stared at Angus.

"Don't say it, I know," Angus said. "I just can't bring myself to confront her. She doesn't strike me as a killer, much less having the physical strength or heart to bury the body in such a cruel manner."

"I don't know. Did you know she used to compete in triathlons back in her day? We can't rule her out."

Angus sighed deeply.

"I just don't think she has it in her to kill someone. Besides, with Daniel being in the condition he's in at the moment, I don't think she'll go anywhere. We'll circle back to her if our other leads run dead."

"It's your call, Sheriff. What about Daniel? Or Bill? He could have been the jealous friend. There could have even been a love triangle."

"You watch too many soap operas, Miguel. I confronted Bill yesterday. He was very proud of the fact that he had discovered Kim. Called her his best asset. I found out from Lily-Mae at Blooms flower shop that the Birch Lane house was a gift from the two men to Kim. That's why it's not registered anywhere. The two of them built most of the town. They could have easily built that house off the books. When

I accused Bill of killing her out of jealousy, he nearly had a fit. Claims he had nothing to do with her death. But here's the interesting thing about that statement; when I accused him, he didn't hesitate denying having anything to do with her death. But, the way he said it. It was as if he had known all along that she was dead. I never mentioned that we identified the body in the barrel to be Kim's. In fact, I only told you guys and Patty yesterday, no one else knows. There's no way he could have known she was dead unless he knew it back then and I strongly doubt Patty would have told him."

"That makes him our prime suspect now. If he knew she was dead, he could be our killer."

Angus stared into the space next to Miguel.

"But you're not convinced, are you?" he asked when he noticed the look in Angus' eyes.

"I'm not ruling him out. After what happened yesterday, Bill Baxter strikes me as someone who is willing to do just about anything for money. Even kill his business partner and that partner's lover."

"Why do I sense there's a but coming?"

Angus dropped his head back onto his pillow.

"Because something just doesn't add up. If Bill was the jealous friend in your love triangle theory, why kill the woman you love and not the man standing in your way of happiness?"

Miguel scratched his head.

"Well, if it isn't the Digbys, and it isn't Bill, who else would have had a good enough reason to kill Kim

Kincaid?" Miguel questioned, looking more confused than ever.

"That's what we're going to find out, even if it takes us another sixteen years to do it."

Eager to get out of the hospital and back onto the case, Angus watched the painstakingly slow droplets of fluid working their way from the IV bag into his arm before he spoke.

"I guess an important question is, who would have been strong enough to lift her body into a barrel, possibly move it to the Birch house, and have the knowledge and physical ability to bury it under gallons of cement without being seen?"

CHAPTER THIRTY-FIVE

Patty straightened the comforter on top of her bed and smoothed the edges into neat corners. She stared at the side Daniel usually slept on, realizing he might never sleep next to her again. Sadness tormented her soul once again. If only she had been more forgiving, more loving toward him, and been the kind of wife he'd always longed for perhaps things could have been different. They'd squandered the past two decades of their marriage, taken it for granted. They had stopped talking and stopped working at making each other happy. She should have tried harder. She should have forgiven him.

Her hand smoothed over his pillow. What was done was done and there was no turning back. The sooner she made peace with that the better. There was too much that was left unsaid between them, and time was no longer on their side. Shutting her eyes, she asked God to forgive her for not putting more effort into their marriage. She asked God to not let Daniel die before she had a chance to say goodbye.

She wiped the tears from her cheeks and smoothed out her hair. You'll be okay, she told herself, then picked up her favorite string of pearls from her dressing table.

As she inspected herself in the mirror, she caught the reflection of the metal box. She'd forgotten all about it. She pulled it from where she had hidden it under the bed. If she were to move on with her life, put the past behind her, she needed to find closure, and deal with whatever was inside that box. Perhaps she would find the answers she'd been searching for all this time. Perhaps the contents would help her understand why Daniel was unfaithful, would help her find peace, would help her set him free.

Urgency to break into the box ripped through her and she grabbed the box off the bed and hurried into the kitchen, dropping it noisily on the kitchen table. In one of the drawers where Daniel kept a few emergency utility tools, she found a large screwdriver. Her heart pounded as her grip tightened on the handle. For a few moments she just stood there, staring at the box, screwdriver in hand as if she were about to stab the box to death. Fear of what she might find inside took up every corner of her heart. Like Pandora's box, there would be no turning back once it was open. But how could she live out her days without knowing?

Just do it. Open the box, she told herself.

Needing no more deliberation, Patty jabbed the tip of the screwdriver between the lock and the box, wedging the thick steel shaft between the two metals. It took several attempts to find the right angle and at one point, she nearly gave up, but she was determined. She needed to know what Daniel had hidden inside.

From deep inside her belly, she grunted and forced all her strength into breaking off the lock. One. More. Try.

The latch burst away from the rest of the box and dropped onto the floor at her feet. Nerves exploded into the pit of her stomach.

Drawing in a deep breath, she moved a shaky hand onto the lid and tried to open it. The lid didn't budge due to years of corrosion. She turned the box on its side and once more used the screwdriver. With little effort, the lid sprung open. She flipped the box right side up again. A final burst of courage removed all hesitation and Patty yanked open the lid, laying bare the full contents of the box.

Her heart skipped two beats before it seemed to stop and her breath caught in her throat.

Answers to questions she never knew to ask slapped cold hands across her face.

There, in the bottom of the box, taunting her, reminding her of what Daniel had done, reminding her of her own personal failures, was a grainy photo of Kim and Daniel leaning up against his stupid little red car, with Daniel looking happier than she'd ever seen. Alongside it, was a grainy black and white ultrasound photo of a fetus and a lock of light brown hair, neatly bound to the photo with a baby blue lace ribbon.

Patty slammed shut the lid and wanted to desperately pretend she hadn't opened the box. She wished she could unsee what was inside that box. Her heart shattered and broke into a million tiny pieces and her body trembled in reaction to the emotions that erupted like a flaming volcano inside her.

Her chest tightened, sucking her breath from her lungs. The walls closed in, threatening to tumble down on top of her. Adrenaline coursed through her and she ran out onto the porch, desperate for air, desperate to get away from everything that reminded her of Daniel.

Suddenly it all made perfect sense. Why Daniel chose Kim over her, why he would never have been happy staying married to her. Because no matter how many times she tried to conceive, Patty Richardson could never give her husband the son he had always longed for.

CHAPTER THIRTY-SIX

P atty's gaze was fixed on the woman who sat at the table on the other side of the café. She'd had a clear view of the couple from the instant they stepped inside. At first, she thought her mind was playing tricks on her, that she was still in shock, delirious. But after closely watching the woman for the past thirty minutes, she knew it wasn't a hallucination.

She was there, sitting on the far side of the café, enjoying a meal with another one of her male victims. There was no mistaking it. It was Kim Kincaid. The same woman who had lured her husband away from her. Who gave Daniel what she never could.

Angus had told her the body in the barrel was Kim, but he was wrong. She was alive and she was back, right there in Weyport. Sitting in the same coffee shop Patty had escaped to in order to clear her head, to get away from the box. It was as if the universe just couldn't let it go and had to torture her until there was nothing left of her soul. To ruin the last moments she had left with Daniel. To steal him away from her once again, as if it wasn't enough for her back then.

Anger welled up in Patty's heart. All these years she had managed to suppress it, pushed it aside. But now, seeing that woman sitting there, holding hands with another feeble fool who had fallen for her deadly charms, the anger walled up like a tidal wave.

She was suffocating in hatred. Her spirit was at war, her soul in torment, her faith in the balance. She couldn't forgive, not anymore.

Patty slammed her coffee cup to the table, spilling half the contents. That woman had taken what could have been her and Daniel's best years. She had robbed her of her marriage, cheated her out of experiencing true joy. No more. Not as long as she still had breath inside her quivering body. She will not let her get away with it again.

Before she knew it, Patty was on her feet, shoulders back, and head held high. With clenched fists by her sides, Patty marched over to the small table in the corner of the café, her eyes pinned to Kim's face. When she stopped next to them, she looked directly into Kim's eyes.

The woman looked up, a curious look in her eyes when their gazes met. Patty's tongue wedged inside her mouth, stopping her from speaking. Heat radiated up into her face as she stood there.

"Can I help you with something, Ma'am?" The woman invited Patty to speak.

A fresh wave of anger burst into Patty's chest. The gall! She knew exactly who she was!

When the words finally came, there was no stopping them, like a fissure in a dam wall, opening little by little until it burst apart, releasing gallons of water.

"How could you do that to me?" Patty's voice was charged with an anger she never knew she possessed.

The startled woman looked at her with confusion.

"Sorry, I don't know what you're talking about."

Wrath exploded from Patty's mouth.

"You know what you did, you evil woman!" Patty shouted. "Everyone in this town knows what you did! How you even have the audacity to show your face here is beyond me!" Patty turned to face the man who sat next to Kim. "Get as far away from this woman as you can. Take it from me. Go back to your wife, save your marriage. This woman is nothing but an opportunistic home wrecker!"

Patty felt as if her heart was breaking all over again. Like the first time she'd found out about their affair, but now compounded knowing they had a son. And the pain was unbearable.

Her legs threatened to give away underneath her quivering body and she held onto the table to stop herself from falling over. But what she couldn't stop, didn't want to stop, were the words she had waited all these years to say.

"You despicable, evil Delilah! You destroyed my

marriage! You took everything from me. I hate you, Kim Kincaid! I HATE YOU!"

As she spat out the words she had fought so hard to keep locked away for decades, she collapsed into a nearby chair, buried her face in her hands, and allowed her tears to wash away what was left of the prison walls she had built around her heart.

Lost in what seemed like an eternity of misery, Patty cried and cried until she begged for God to let her die instead. Kim could have Daniel, share the life they always wanted, live happily ever after. All she wanted now was to be let out of her misery.

Desperate to be set free from the agony, she let go of the hope of having a life with Daniel, stopped fighting for something she now knew she would never have.

From across the table, the woman reached out and touched Patty's hand while she spoke in a gentle voice.

"You must be Patty Richardson. I'm Vanessa, Kim was my identical twin sister."

The words seemed to echo in the quiet coffee shop. Battered and bruised from a lifetime of anguish that had held her captive in a void between forgiveness and hate, Patty raised her head and stared into the woman's face. Her eyes were gentle, kind, and compassionate.

"Kim was my sister," she repeated, reaching across the table with a single photo in her hands.

"See, that's us, taken a few months before she disappeared. It was the last time I saw her alive."

Vanessa's voice trailed off as sadness and pity overcame her.

"I'm so sorry Kim did this to you. I'm so deeply sorry, Patty," Vanessa whispered, leaning into Rowley's side.

Patty stared at the photo, tears still pooled in her eyes. Their appearance truly was identical.

"I don't know what to say," Patty said after a while.

Vanessa's hand reached for hers again.

"It's okay. It seems no one in Weyport knew," Vanessa replied. "I feel like I need to apologize for what my sister did, to you and to the entire town."

Patty pulled a tissue from her sleeve and wiped her eyes before blowing her nose.

"I didn't mean...I'm sorry I said those evil things to you. I was just so angry when I saw you here. I thought you were her."

"I would have done the same thing if I had been in your shoes. At least this explains why everyone's been so unfriendly toward me. The whispering and the staring. They all think I'm Kim."

Patty nodded. "You look exactly like her."

Vanessa nodded.

"I know. I was shocked too when I met her for the first time. I only found out I had a twin seventeen years ago. I never really got to know her. I didn't know what she did to you, the damage she did, and the hurt she caused you."

"Not just to me. Most of the women in this town couldn't stand the sight of her. Your sister was quite the seductress. My Daniel was just foolish enough to fall for her devious wiles."

Vanessa paused.

"I'd like to meet your husband, if that's okay with you."

Patty shrugged her shoulders.

"It won't do you any good. He's in a coma, in the hospital. The doctors don't think he'll make it."

"I'm sorry to hear that but if there's any chance he could hear me I'd still like to talk with him, please. I need to do this."

Vanessa's eyes were urgent, pleading, as if she too needed closure.

Patty nodded.

"I guess we all need to find a way to move on, so if this is what you need, I won't stop you."

"Thank you," Vanessa replied. "We have some paperwork to take care of at the county office but it shouldn't take long. We can meet you at the hospital in a little while."

CHAPTER THIRTY-SEVEN

B y the time lunch rolled around, Angus had been discharged from hospital and was already back behind his desk. Miguel had joined the search for Bill, who was still at large, and Tammy had miraculously managed to confirm all the information that had come to light in the past twenty-four hours.

As Angus pored over the case files, one detailing Kim's disappearance sixteen years ago, and the second one pertaining to the details of the discovery of her body, he couldn't ignore the strong hunch that he was missing a crucial piece of information. He rolled his chair back from his desk and lingered, his eyes never leaving the photos of Kim's corpse taken at the Birch Lane house. She was placed feet first in the barrel, not headfirst. Someone would have had to pick her up in order to lower her into the keg in this manner. Even if the barrel was tipped on its side and the body was pushed in from the ground it would have been too heavy to tip upright again. Kim was of average height and, having physically seen her identical twin, could not have been lifted by a woman.

Angus jumped up, sending his chair rolling back against the wall as it struck him.

There had to have been at least two people involved.

He picked up the photos and hurried into the conference room where he stuck them onto the evidence board.

Having seen him rush by her desk, Tammy followed Angus into the room.

"What's up? Have you found something?"

"Let me run something by you, Tammy. You're about the same build and height as Patty Richardson, right?"

"I'd say so, yes. Why?"

He pointed to the photos on the board.

"Would you be able to lift an unconscious body into a steel keg like this, placing her feet first, all by yourself?"

Tammy contemplated the question.

"I don't think I could do that with a ten-year-old, much less an adult woman."

"How about if the keg was on its side and the body slid in from the ground? Would you be able to lift it into an upright position again?"

Tammy shook her head.

"Not a chance."

Angus looked at her, a wide grin on his face.

"We're not looking for one killer. We're looking for at

least two suspects. Two people who knew each other, who would have both benefited from Kim Kincaid's death."

"Surely you can't be thinking Patty had anything to do with this," Tammy said with surprise.

"It pains me to have to even consider her, Tammy, but who else? Her husband was having an affair. She was being laughed at by the entire town, disgraced and judged. Who in their sound mind can endure such humiliation? She had motive, opportunity, and the means. But here's the thing. I think Bill Baxter helped her. That's the only way I can explain how he already knew Kim was dead and why he was so defensive when I accused him of killing her. It would be why he felt he needed to kill Patty yesterday. I think Patty could have killed Kim then asked Bill to help dispose of the body. She couldn't have done it on her own. And what better way to hide Kim's body than in the foundation of her own house? A house Bill and Daniel had built for Kim off the books. Bill's entire business was at stake if Daniel ran off with Kim. He nearly killed Patty at the house yesterday. It could have been a deliberate effort to cover up his tracks."

"I suppose you could be right, but I just cannot wrap my head around Patty having the guts to kill someone. She's pedantic about safety in the neighborhood, a real stickler for justice. Bill Baxter on the other hand, I don't trust him as far as I can throw him. But Patty Richardson?"

Angus rubbed the back of his head.

"I know, I'm having a hard time with it too. She's been

nothing but kind and warm to me since the day I got here, and we've shared a few special moments of late. But we have a job to do and sometimes that job gets in the way of relationships. We cannot allow our judgment to be clouded. We follow the evidence and look at the facts, that's what we do. That's how it has to be."

"What if you're wrong? If you accuse her, she might never forgive you, you know."

Angus couldn't think of that now. The thought of hurting Patty after learning how she felt about him stabbed at his conscience. But he had a job to do, a killer to catch, and a case to close. If he was wrong, he'd face the music—or her wrath.

Just then Miguel came rushing in.

"We found him, Sheriff. Bill Baxter's in custody. He's refusing to talk without his lawyer present, but I have him waiting in the interrogation room, nonetheless. I thought you might want to have a go at him and see if you can get him to confess before his lawyer gets here."

"Great job, Miguel." Angus turned to Tammy. "I guess we will soon find out if I'm right. In the meantime, we need to make sure we keep an eye on Patty, just in case I'm right. Round up a couple of deputies and station them outside her house. Tell them, if she asks, they are to inform her that they're only there to make sure she's safe. We don't want to give her any reason to run. They need to stick to her like glue and report back. Got it?"

"10-4, Sheriff," Tammy said and left.

"What did I miss?" asked Miguel.

"I'll fill you in on the way but hopefully we can get Bill to spill the beans, before I do something I'm probably going to regret for the rest of my life."

IN THE INTERROGATION ROOM, Bill's body language spoke volumes. His lips were pursed together, his arms were crossed, and he sat sideways in his chair. Angus knew he'd have to approach him with care.

"Sorry to keep you waiting, Mr. Baxter," Angus started.

Bill rolled his eyes then gazed at the sling around Angus' arm.

"Yeah, I survived. Turns out I was really lucky," Angus said, then paused. "Unlike you, I'm afraid. You've gotten yourself in a real pickle here."

Again, Angus paused, hoping Bill would say something. He didn't.

"Look Bill, we can dance around the subject all day, but you know as well as I do there's no chance of you walking away scot-free. Your wife's going to have to get used to the idea of you not being around for a long while."

Something in Bill's eyes flickered and he crossed his legs with meaning.

He had struck a nerve, Angus thought.

"Your wife doesn't know, does she?"

Bill rolled his eyes again.

"Or she does, and she's already kicked you out."

This time Bill snickered.

Angus pushed the writing pad and pen across the desk.

"Tell me how you did it, how you killed Kim Kincaid."

Bill's brow furrowed then he finally spoke.

"I already told you. I wasn't the one who killed her. Now, save yourself a lot of time and effort because I'm not saying anything else without my lawyer present."

Something about the way Bill said it, his tone, his facial expression - something hinted that Bill knew exactly who killed Kim Kincaid.

Angus lingered in his chair, his mind working frantically through the clues as he studied Bill's face.

Moments later he jumped up, as if the chair had burned his seat. He snatched the pen and pad off the desk, startling both Bill and Miguel and rushed out.

"What's happening?" Miguel called after him. "Where are we going?"

But Angus didn't answer, his mind too focused on what lay ahead.

CHAPTER THIRTY-EIGHT

When Patty arrived at the hospital, she found Belinda Baxter waiting for her outside Daniel's room.

"Oh, thank heavens you're here, Patty. I've been looking for you everywhere. I went by the house, and you weren't there."

"What do you want, Belinda?" Patty asked.

"I was hoping we could talk."

"There's nothing left to talk about. Your husband did quite enough of that already."

Patty pushed past Belinda and entered the room where she propped her purse on the chair next to Daniel's bed.

"I heard. I don't know what came over Bill yesterday. He's just so desperate to save his company. This feud with Daniel and the breakup of their business, well, things have

229

never been the same since. He owes a lot of money to a lot of investors and—"

"Save it, Belinda, I'm not interested. Bill nearly killed me yesterday. He tied me up like an animal. If it weren't for Angus, who, by the way, Bill shot, I would be dead. Trust me, nothing you say to me right now will remedy that so please, just leave."

Belinda moved to the foot of the bed.

"Please, Patty, I'm sorry. Like I said, I don't know what came over him. I don't even know where Bill is. He never came home last night. For all I know he's finally plucked up the courage to leave me too. He's been bored with me for years now. But us, we've always been there for each other. You and I, together, we've been friends since college. Even when Daniel and Bill had their falling out, our friendship survived. I've always been there for you, and I want to be there for you now. Let me help you through this terrible time with Daniel," she begged.

Patty turned to look at her. There was nothing timid about Belinda Baxter. She was as strong and dependable as ever. The same as she'd always been, from the moment they met back in college, after Patty's assault. If it hadn't been for Belinda, she might not have emotionally survived the ordeal.

But things were different now. Everything had changed. She had changed. All she wanted to do was move on, put the past behind her, heal.

"Please, Patty, let me help you. You shouldn't have to

go through this on your own. We've always been there for each other. We can get through this, start over."

"What if I don't want you to, Belinda? Have you stopped to think about that? What if all I want is to be left alone with my husband before I have to switch off these machines and watch him die. Think about that for one minute. I don't need him, and I don't need you!"

Patty watched as the effect of her words took shape in Belinda's eyes. They hurt her and were harsh, she knew, but they were true. She didn't need anyone's pity, didn't want to be reminded of the love she never had.

"You don't mean that," Belinda said, her voice heavy with emotion. "I know you, Patty Richardson, and this isn't the real you. You're too weak to handle this on your own. You were never good at getting through crisis on your own. But I'm here, like I've always been. You need me."

"Well, meet the new me then and get used to her. Because this Patty is never going to allow anyone to hurt her ever again. Now leave, Belinda. Go find your husband and give him all your attention. I don't need it and I don't want it."

Just then there was a quiet knock on the door behind them.

"Is it okay to come in?"

It was Vanessa. She was alone, standing in the doorway.

"Belinda was just leaving," Patty announced, her voice stern as she beckoned for Vanessa to come in.

Belinda didn't respond, her face as white as the sheets on the bed.

When Vanessa went to stand on the other side of the bed next to Daniel, merely feet away from her, Belinda's entire demeanor changed.

Suddenly all that had held Belinda together in a neat, dependable package was slowly coming apart.

"It can't be! You can't be alive, it's impossible!"

Patty tried to say something, but Belinda was already beside herself. Vanessa tried taking a few steps toward her, to introduce herself, but Belinda didn't want to hear it.

"No! Stay away!"

Belinda reached inside her purse and before anyone could say anything she pulled out a handgun.

Patty shrieked, took two steps back and fell noisily against the bedside cabinet.

"Have you finally lost your mind, Belinda? Put that thing away before you hurt someone," Patty yelled.

But Belinda's aim remained fixed on Vanessa, both her hands gripping the gun, holding it steady.

Vanessa opened her mouth to scream.

"Don't even think about it!" Belinda stopped her, forcing Vanessa to stifle the screams with her hands over her mouth.

Belinda's face held nothing but hatred as she stared at Vanessa.

"You evil woman!" Belinda shouted at Vanessa; the gun now aimed directly at her face.

Vanessa cowered down onto the floor next to the bed.

"Belinda, you're making a mistake," Patty tried to reason with her.

But Belinda's eyes had lost all sanity and tenderness.

Vanessa's whimpering turned to crying, one hand stretched out over the side of the bed, begging for Belinda not to shoot her.

"Belinda, put the gun down! What are you doing?" Patty yelled from where she was taking cover behind the steel bedside table.

"I'm not going to let this woman ruin your life again! She won't get away with it a second time. This time I'll make sure she's dead!"

Stunned at Belinda's words, Patty's mind tried to make sense of what she had just heard.

"What are you talking about?" Patty asked, starting to panic.

Belinda's angry eyes darted to Patty's questioning gaze.

"I told you. We're friends. There's nothing I won't do for you. Nothing."

"But this? Friends don't pull guns on people. Just put it down, okay? Let's talk about this. You're making a big mistake. This isn't Kim."

Belinda's eyes went wild with rage, her body moving slowly around the bed to where she now had nothing standing between her and Vanessa.

"Belinda, please, stop. You've got this all wrong," Patty

begged when Belinda pointed the gun firmly toward Vanessa's head.

"I told you; I'm here to take care of you, Patty. I don't know how she survived it or who they found in the barrel, but this time I'll make sure she's dead."

Patty's brow furrowed.

"You killed Kim?"

"Apparently not. I should have hit her over the head harder and made sure she was dead before he buried her."

"What are you saying?" Patty asked, becoming desperate for answers.

"She hurt you, Patty. She stole your husband. I wasn't going to let that happen, especially after she told me Daniel was going to divorce you so they could get married. Not after watching you go through the agony of your miscarriages just to give Daniel a child. And the pain when the doctors told you you'd never be able to carry to term. You became useless to Daniel. I couldn't let them hurt you like that. So, I did what needed to be done, what any loyal friend would do. I took care of it."

"You killed and buried Kim," Patty stated the obvious, still unwilling to believe her ears.

"I went to her house and confronted her. I even offered her money to disappear, but you wouldn't, would you, Kim?" Belinda said to Vanessa. "You should have just taken the money and left Weyport. But no, you came at me with that hammer and left me no choice. And as usual Bill made a mess of it. He was supposed to bury you. So how did you do it huh, Kim? Did you use your charm to get him to let you go? Was my husband next on your list or were you already sleeping with him, too?"

Belinda took aim to shoot the woman she thought was Kim.

A single gunshot echoed through the quiet room.

Vanessa squealed.

Patty screamed.

Belinda fell sideways across the bed, draped over Daniel's feet, shrieking in pain as she clutched her arm to her chest.

When Patty looked where the shot came from, she spotted Angus in the doorway, smoke wafting from the tip of his gun.

CHAPTER THIRTY-NINE

A ngus wrapped his arm around Patty, and pulled her close until her body stopped shaking.

"You're safe now, Patty," he whispered.

Patty clung to him and the safety he provided.

"It's all over, they can't hurt you anymore. The two of them will be going to prison for a very long time."

Patty's eyes met his.

"I still can't believe it, Angus. I can't believe they were capable of doing something so evil. I thought I knew them."

"People do strange things for love and money, and when those two evils take over, they choke out the hearts of the people you thought you once knew."

"How did I not see it though? Belinda and I have been friends for so long. Was I so wrapped up in my own problems that I stopped paying attention to her?"

"There's no way you could have known or stopped it. Belinda's loyalty toward your friendship went a bit too far. But, as twisted as it was, she thought she was doing the right thing to protect her friend. She cared for you, and maybe loved too hard. And Bill, he did what he thought he needed to do to protect his wife no matter what. Misguided loyalty is what this was. We protect those we love; it's human nature. It's when the lines between good and evil get blurred that we need to stop and choose which side we're on."

Patty's eyes went to Daniel where he lay quietly in his bed, unaware of what had just happened.

"I don't know how I'm going to do this, Angus. I don't know how I'm supposed to grant them permission to turn off those machines. All these years I wanted to hate him with every cell in my body. But now, seeing him here like this, all I want to do is love him."

"It sounds to me like you might have forgiven him."

She smiled.

"Forgiveness comes easy when you realize you love someone. It's a choice, not an option."

She got up and walked over to his bedside and planted a gentle kiss on Daniel's forehead.

"Perhaps true forgiveness lies in letting go," Patty whispered next to Daniel's ear. "I have to let it all go, Daniel. All the pain, all the guilt, all the shame, I'm letting it all go. I've never stopped loving you, and I never will, Daniel Richardson."

When Patty had said what needed to be said, she found the peace she had longed for and never thought she would find. She turned and faced Angus.

"I think I'm ready to let him go now," she whispered.

Angus nodded, thankful that God had shown her how to forgive and grateful that she'd found the strength to let go.

Together they went in search of the doctor and found him in his office, clicking away at his computer. Patty stood in the doorway, Angus' arm holding her steady.

"I'm ready to sign those papers now," she said quietly.

The doctor stood up, his eyebrows raised as his eyes glimmered with excitement.

"I don't think that's going to be necessary, Mrs. Richardson."

His gaze went to a corner of his office where Vanessa and Rowley Digby were seated at a round table, filling out forms. Seated across from them a young man watched them. The close resemblance between him and Daniel was undeniable.

Patty gasped, knowing instantly that he was Daniel and Kim's son. She hesitated, unable to move, not knowing if she wanted to.

The doctor stepped out from behind his desk and hurried toward her.

"I think we might have found a way to save your husband," he said.

Patty didn't respond. Her eyes were glued to the young man who had Daniel's eyes and his smile.

"Patty," Vanessa spoke gently as she rose from behind the table. "This is Danny, Daniel's son."

Patty just stood there, staring into the eyes of the son she could never give Daniel. His eyes were warm and his hair was the same color Daniel's used to be before it turned white.

"We ran some tests. Danny's DNA is a match to your husband's, Mrs. Richardson," the doctor announced. "He's agreed to a bone marrow transplant. We're still running a few more tests but I am confident the outcome will be positive. We could have them both prepped and ready by this evening."

Patty's eyes drifted to the doctor's face then back to Danny's.

"I'd like to do this for my father. He deserves to have another chance at life," Danny said.

Vanessa walked toward Patty and closed her hands over Patty's.

"We can't erase what my sister did. We can't take away all the hurt she caused you, but we can help save Daniel's life, Patty. We can do what's right."

Patty snatched her hands away, turned, and ran out the room, as fast as her legs would carry her. She needed to run, needed to get away, needed to breathe.

Angus rushed after her and eventually caught up with her near a large window that overlooked the courtyard.

"Patty, what's wrong?" he asked with tenderness, his hand on her shoulder.

She just shook her head, her eyes sad and filled with confusion.

"It's going to be okay," Angus consoled as the tears now ran freely down her cheeks.

"He looks just like him. Danny looks exactly like Daniel."

"I'm sorry you had to find out like this," Angus whispered.

Patty pulled away from him.

"I didn't. I found out yesterday."

Angus frowned.

"The box. There was an ultrasound picture and a lock of hair in the box. I must have forgotten about it, but I remember a man coming to our house one night looking for Daniel. I'd never seen him before. Later, I found out that he was a private investigator that Daniel had hired to find Kim. It was about a year or so after her disappearance. The investigator gave Daniel an envelope, which upset him terribly. That night, everything changed between us. He changed. It was as if he had died inside. I had assumed it might have been a letter from Kim telling him she wasn't coming back. But now I think it might have been what he'd been hiding in that box all this time. He knew Kim was pregnant and knew he had a son. All these years, he knew. If I agree to this and Daniel wakes up, he'll want a relationship with his son, and it'll be a constant reminder of what he did all those years ago. I don't know if I can do it, if I can relive the past."

Angus found her gaze.

"You never had a son, Patty. The way I see it, God is presenting you with an opportunity to fill that void, to extend the love you have for Daniel to his son. You could allow Christ to restore your relationship and to wipe the slate clean. Forget the past; bury all you chose to let go of when you stood next to his bed a few minutes ago. Allow God to make all things new and to revive what you once longed for. God is there in the whispers but He's also in the shout. He knows what you need and He's ready to give it to you. Let Him."

Deciding that it was best to give her time on her own, he gave her a gentle hug and then left.

But Patty already knew what she needed to do.

So, later that night, when Patty and Vanessa watched from behind a large window as Daniel and his son lay side-by-side in their hospital room, God gave Patty a new revelation. As she watched the fluid run through the tubes that were draped between father and son, transferring new life into Daniel's body, she knew that God had been at work all along. Like oil in a lamp feeding a flame, burning new life into his spirit, Daniel's oil was being replenished and purified, like currents of living water, bringing new hope into being.

And as the Holy Spirit did what needed to be done,

Patty found true freedom. The kind that came when one realigned with Christ. God was pouring out His grace and mercy, bringing with it forgiveness, healing, and second chances. And as Daniel's new oil fused with his body, surging new life into his spirit, she knew her old life was gone too and that a new, brighter one was emerging.

And she was finally ready for it.

"Therefore, if anyone is in Christ, he is a new creation; old things have passed away; behold, all things have become new."

- 2 Corinthians 5:17 -

THANK you for reading *DANIEL'S OIL*. New clues about his brother come to light when Angus Reid's journey continues in a brand new page-turning mystery in book 3, ***CALEB'S CROSS***, coming early 2024!

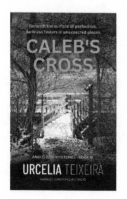

A deadly secret from Caleb Townsend's past threatens to destroy his perfect reputation. As he tries to keep it hidden, mystery unravels and soon picks off its victims, one at a time.

Please consider leaving a review of Daniel's Oil. I'd love to know if you solved the

mystery before you reached the end.

Want updates? Join my Reader Community (newsletter.urcelia.com/signup)

MORE BOOKS BY URCELIA TEIXEIRA

Angus Reid Mysteries series
Jacob's Well
Daniel's Oil
Caleb's Cross

Adam Cross series
Every Good Gift
Every Good Plan
Every Good Work

Jorja Rose trilogy
Vengeance is Mine
Shadow of Fear
Wages of Sin

Alex Hunt series
The Papua Incident (FREE!)
The Rhapta Key
The Gilded Treason
The Alpha Strain
The Dauphin Deception
The Bari Bones
The Caiaphas Code

PICK A BUNDLE FOR MASSIVE SAVINGS exclusive to my online
store!
Save up to 50% off plus get an additional 10% discount coupon.
Visit https://shop.urcelia.com

More books coming soon! Sign up to my newsletter to be notified of new releases, giveaways and pre-release specials.

MESSAGE FROM THE AUTHOR

All glory be to the Lord, my God who breathed every word through me onto these pages.

*I have put my words in your mouth and
covered you with the shadow of My hand
Isaiah 51:16*

It is my sincere prayer that you not only enjoyed the story, but drew courage, inspiration, and hope from it, just as I did while writing it. Thank you sincerely, for reading *JACOB'S WELL.*

I appreciate your help in spreading the word, including telling a friend. Reviews help readers find books! Please leave a review on your favorite book site.

ABOUT THE AUTHOR

Award winning author of faith-filled Christian Suspense
Thrillers that won't let you go!™

Urcelia Teixeira, writes gripping Christian mystery,
thriller and suspense novels that will keep you on the edge
of your seat! Firm in her Christian faith, all her books are
free from profanity and unnecessary sexually suggestive
scenes.

She made her writing debut in December 2017,
kicking off her newly discovered author journey with her
fast-paced archaeological adventure thriller novels that
readers have described as 'Indiana Jones meets Lara Croft
with a twist of Bourne.'

But, five novels in, and nearly eighteen months later,
she had a spiritual re-awakening, and she wrote the sixth
and final book in her Alex Hunt Adventure Thriller series.
She now fondly refers to *The Caiaphas Code* as her
redemption book. Her statement of faith. And although
this series has reached multiple Amazon Bestseller lists,
she took the bold step of following her true calling and

switched to writing what honors her Creator: Christian Mystery and Suspense fiction.

The first book in her newly discovered genre went on to win the 2021 Illumination Awards Silver medal in the Christian Fiction category and the series reached multiple Amazon Bestseller lists!

While this success is a great honor and blessing, all glory goes to God alone who breathed every word through her!

A committed Christian for over twenty years, she now lives by the following mantra:

"I used to be a writer. Now I am a writer with a purpose!"

For more on Urcelia and her books, visit https://www.urcelia.com

To walk alongside her as she deepens her writing journey and walks with God, sign up to her Newsletter - https://newsletter.urcelia.com/signup

or

Follow her at

goodreads.com/urcelia_teixeira

facebook.com/urceliateixeira

bookbub.com/authors/urcelia-teixeira

amazon.com/author/urceliateixeira

instagram.com/urceliateixeira

pinterest.com/urcelia_teixeira

Made in United States
Orlando, FL
26 September 2023

37307685R00157